I0687588

Ex-Treme Measures

by

Mickey J Corrigan

Ex-Treme Measures

Contact Information: info@thewildrosepress.com

Cover Art by *Diana Carlile*

The Wild Rose Press, Inc.
PO Box 708
Adams Basin, NY 14410-0708

Visit us at www.thewildrosepress.com

Publishing History
First Edition, 2015
Print ISBN 978-1-5092-0341-3
Digital ISBN 978-1-5092-0342-0

Published in the United States of America

Men. **You can't live with them.**
You can't kill them... Or can you?

My assistant Ringo and I sat in the middle of the room at a small table for two. The crowd surged around us. The men were mostly middle-aged or older, the women under fifty and hungry.

We were out of place, but then again, we usually are. Ringo and I frequent the Tam in order to troll for clients. And to get a buzz on. Our version of foreplay.

Sometimes the need for our services made me sad. Why were men and women so mismatched? Our bodies are designed for love. Humans are drawn to coupling, forming pairs bonded for both sexual and social reasons. Yet, the male tends to lose interest and is likely to wander. Knowing this is true throughout the animal kingdom doesn't make it any easier to accept.

And for those who cannot accept, Ringo and I offer our special domestic relations elimination services. Too bad my business couldn't become obsolete, with no need for Ringo and me to do what we've learned to do best.

"You'd look great in something from the Secret," my assistant said, apropos of nothing but several pints aswirl in the male brain. "Something firehouse red. Made out of see-through silk, short and sweet. And maybe edible." He paused, licked his wet lips. "Definitely edible."

We stared at one another. My assistant's charcoal eyes smoldered. I sighed. I knew enough about men to say, "Fine. We can talk about our business crises later."

His joy was childlike, and I loved him for that. But only for the night. I love my men one at a time, but never forever. I advise all my clients to do the same.

Nobody ever listens to me on this.

Dedication

To all my divorced and
almost-divorced friends...if only.

Prologue

"I don't care what it costs. I want that man dead."

Mrs. Boscoe's perfectly sculpted face pinkened. Her soft voice rose in pitch. I could tell she meant what she'd said. I'd been in the game long enough to be able to separate the Chicken Littles from the cash cows. Killing scumbag husbands was a dirty business, but a lucrative one. I had blood and grime beneath my unpolished nails. Still, being a hitwoman paid the bills.

Turning aside for a moment to face the slim laptop on my desk, I tapped on the keyboard and pulled up the standard private investigations release contract. After sending it to print, I told my new client, "I'll need you to sign this before you pay the retainer fee." I kept my voice even, steady. To help the client remain calm. This was make it or break it time. I held my breath while the printer whirred.

After I slid the form across my clean glass desk, I watched Mrs. Boscoe. She skimmed the legalese. Her tastefully bleached hair formed a solid yellow curtain that hid her finely boned model's face. Her manicure was French, the breasts perky saline. The tight taupe skirt a recent Dior, the perfume old-time Chanel. Of course, the shoes were Jimmy Choo, the bag Prada. I was used to her type, rich bitches from the spoiled island of Palm Beach. Still, I was on her side. One hundred percent.

My newest client handed me the signed contract and a deposit of five thousand dollars. Her salon-tanned hand shook as she counted out the bills. "What happens next, Ms. Treme?"

"Now you go home and slip into something more comfortable," I advised. "Your job for the next month is to have as much sex with your husband as you can stand. Lounge around in your filmiest teddies. Mix him his favorite cocktails. Make him his favorite meals. Do whatever he asks, and do it with a smile. Try to get away on vacation. See if you can convince him to fly to Bora Bora with you. Or Paris. Buy new lingerie. Get a bikini wax, a Botox treatment." She winced. "This is the last ditch stage. Sometimes it actually works."

One time it worked. But I don't tell my clients the odds. It's too discouraging.

"Whatever happens, be sure to call your friends and tell them how wonderful everything is," I continued. "Tell everyone you've fallen back in love. Kiss him on the lips when you're out in public. Hold his hand in restaurants. Throw yourself at him in front of the staff. Make sure everyone thinks you two are back on track."

She nodded before asking the same question they all ask. "What about that bitch he's sleeping with?"

They always want to know what they should do about the other woman. I tell them all the same thing, but really, it's useless. They can't forget about her. If they could, they wouldn't be here on the mainland, sitting in my office in down and dirty Deport Beach, slut sister city to married-up Palm Beach. If these women could just ignore their rich husbands' dalliances, they wouldn't be paying me the big bucks.

And I wouldn't be ex-terminating their cheating spouses.

"Forget about her," I told Mrs. Boscoe. "You need to focus your energy on your husband. And if he goes for it, if everything works out, I'll be happy for you. So happy I'll refund your money. One hundred percent."

Like I said, that's only happened once. One time in the seven years I've been open for business. Nine months after I refunded that particular retainer fee, the client returned. Now she's the owner of a multimillion dollar real estate company and her husband's six feet under. Where he belongs.

I accompanied Mrs. Boscoe to my office door. She walked with the smooth grace of a runner or ballroom dancer. I would kill for legs like hers. Soon enough, that would be exactly what I would do.

****

Thirty-seven days later, Mr. Boscoe was reported missing. His sixty-foot yacht had sunk off the coast of Bimini. A young woman—not his wife—had been with him at the time. In glittery bistros and gluttonous mansions, Palm Beach tittered over the scandal. In Deport Beach, we snickered over our cardboard cups of take-out coffee.

Ex-Treme Measures is *the* place for Palm Beach wives to outsource revenge. Because I back all my clients. One hundred percent.

Chapter One

"I never thought I would say something like this, but he deserves to die. For what he's done to me, he should be put down. Like a rabid animal."

My new client was breathtaking. Like a middle-aged Christie Brinkley. But her expression betrayed her status—enraged and worn down. They all are when they're on the verge of eliminating the source of their pain, only to find out they have to endure the marital torture for at least another month. None of them want to wait through the required cooling off period. Which is exactly why I require one. I offer a professional service, not the opportunity for self-help justice.

Angry women make mistakes. Ex-Treme Measures does not.

Mrs. Emworth straightened her narrow shoulders and ran a hand through her perfectly coiffed hair. Even on the down side of fifty, the woman radiated sex appeal. The high-end anti-aging doctors had been able to do wonders with her reconstruction. If you start with good bone structure, it's not so difficult to maintain the original beauty. Heads would certainly turn when she walked past. I'm sure men have looked at her with lust and longing all her adult life.

I gave her the usual speech about giving her husband, a multimillionaire and high-visibility attorney type, one last chance to devote himself. Fat chance of that happening. Still, she needed the next few weeks to tamp down her hatred. And make sure she was up for the task she'd hired us to do.

I stood up from my seat at the desk. "See if he can still be the man you married."

It was unlikely, but worth one last effort. It would assuage her guilt later when he was gone.

"Please don't hesitate to call me over the next four weeks," I told her as we walked to my office door. "You have my cell number. Use it. I answer to my clients on a twenty-four/seven basis." I paused, and she looked me in the eye. We were the same height, but she had the extra leverage of a glitzy pair of five-inch cork heels. As I shook her bejeweled hand, I continued. "If I don't hear from you, I will contact you in one month's time. In the interim, do consider all your options. Ex-Treme Measures should be the absolute final measure. Used only as directed and only when necessary."

She didn't smile at this. None of them do at this point. By the time they come to me, these women are almost fully debilitated. Their humor, along with their confidence and self-esteem, has ebbed. If it was low to begin with, now the tide is out. When they've made the decision to resort to Ex-Treme Measures, it's because there's nothing else left.

She'd given him twenty-six years of her life. Two sons. Her youth. Now he was screwing around with someone her boys' age. And soon enough, he would leave her. The way of the male animal. Nature can be a real bitch.

But I didn't say this to Mrs. Emworth. Her depression was palpable. She didn't need me to fill in her blanks.

5

The loss of one's beloved to another woman can lead to a particularly bleak existential state. Betrayed women are emptied of everything. Sucked dry, hollow, soulless. Existing in the aftermath, they're like popped balloons. Emotionally flattened out. Some, however, are refueled by the hot breath of vengeance. These are the women who find their way to my discrete office tucked away in a scattershot neighborhood in west Deport Beach.

I rested my hand on Mrs. Emworth's shoulder, which felt cold and hard under the silk of her Vera Wang blouse. A shirt worth more than a month's rent on my office. I gave her the cooling off speech.

"Before you go, I need to impress upon you the importance of your decision. Do make sure you are fully and consciously aware of the consequences of the choice you are making. Women are not powerless creatures. Men do not deserve to be happy at everyone else's expense. But, once you pass the reins to me, there's no going back. Do you understand?"

My client averted her carefully made-up eyes, but her cheeks flushed. Her smooth skin was flawless, stunning. Either she was of Scandinavian descent or she'd been able to maintain the complexion of a Danish beauty queen with a battery of experimental hormones. Either way, it seemed a shame that a man could pull the rug out from under her. Physical perfection like hers deserved to be worshipped.

There was heat in her voice when she said, "Believe me, Ms. Treme, I get it. I know exactly what I'm doing. My husband's a filthy rotten scumbag. If I let him leave me for that slut—and he will leave me, I'm sure of it. After all, he left his second wife for me when I was young. Around your age, thirty-something."

Here she sighed heavily.

It would be better for business if I were older. The majority of my clients seem to resent my comparable youth. I'm thirty-seven, old enough to get dumped for an updated version. But most of my clients are postmenopausal. They're over the edge emotionally anyway, their hormones rampaging through their aging bodies. A lot of them are borderline crazy, pushed to the boundaries of sanity by estrogen and sagging skin. I do understand how these women feel when their beloved beats a hasty retreat, tail between his legs, but I must admit I cannot empathize. Not fully. Time will change that, of course. It does for us all.

Younger women get cheated on, too, but we're more flexible, more resilient. Women under fifty tend to resurface after a dumping. We try to jump back on board to land ourselves another big fish. Younger women still want to go fishing. Most of my clients, however, are past all that. They would prefer to sit on the dock and age gracefully. They're done with the hunt. They no longer wish to play the game. I can respect that, even if I'm not quite there yet myself.

"If I don't stop him, if I let him leave me," my client continued, "I'll end up with nothing. He's a senior partner in his firm, for god's sake. He'll make sure I can't find decent representation anywhere in Palm Beach. Then he'll pull some crafty move and leave me with some kiss-off cash and the clothes on my back."

This wasn't true, and I'd been through the particulars with her already. As his wife of twenty-plus years, she was entitled to half his assets. But half was never enough, not when you'd been seriously fucked over, heartlessly traded in for a newer model. This wasn't about the money. This was about the heart. I'd been in business long enough to know about routine affluence. I was well aware what women like Mrs. Emworth were after. Unless the leopard changed his dirty spots for virginally clean ones, which was highly unlikely no matter how much she spent at Victoria's Secret, the scorned wife wanted it all. Nothing would do but everything he had.

"I understand, but please try to do your best for the next few weeks. See if you might patch things up. Take it one day at a time." I opened the door and hustled her out in the most gentle manner. "And call me anytime, for any reason."

She thanked me and managed a wan smile. She hid her troubled eyes behind a pair of oversized Gucci shades as she left to face another empty day in a heartless world. Even at her worst, the woman radiated elegance and style. One of the brighter bulbs to light up my office.

Although, I must say, I do work with a lot of high class, well put together women. I'd often thought about how convenient it would have been if I were a man. I might have scored with quite a few of my indebted clients, especially after I completed the job for them. Or, if I were gay, I could have reaped the rewards of having a business that caters to sexually deprived females in the midst of an anti-male life phase. However, I'm one hundred percent straight. Plus, I'm the ultimate professional. I always maintain a professional distance. Which is why I'm still in business. I keep my nose clean and my clients pleased.

Word gets around. Ex-Treme Measures is trustworthy. Discrete. Expensive, but well worth the investment.

All my clients are satisfied clients.

After the lovely and heartbroken Mrs. Finnian Emworth disappeared into the elevator to the lobby, I allowed myself the secret pleasure of a deep, sorrowful sigh. The kind of heartfelt sigh I only allow myself to exhale in private. A sigh full of romantic disappointment and acute pity. My profession can bring on periods of wistfulness and some mild depression. I find it insanely sad that even the most remarkable women cannot find a true and lasting love.

How could this be? Why, in an era of made-to-order beauty and off-the-menu sexuality, would a man choose to cheat on his lovely, devoted wife?

Simple. Because men are unable to control their lustful urges. They're the most base of animals. Driven by the primitive limbic system in their testosterone-fueled brains, men are no better than reptiles. Or hound dogs. Pigs. They'll rut just because they can.

Yet, most females fail to seek retribution, even though they know they can. This is true of animals as well as humans.

The situation may be nature's way, but it certainly seems unfair. That's why Ex-Treme Measures is doing what we can to alter primal, ingrained behaviors. We are here to help our civilization evolve.

At least, that's what I tell myself when I'm wondering why the hell I'm in this wacked business.

****

While I was filing Mrs. Emworth's contract, a boilerplate form delineating the receipt of a retainer fee for unspecified domestic surveillance services to come, my cell buzzed.

Ringo.

I was tempted not to answer. Ringo is my assistant at Ex-Treme Measures, and I rely on him for certain essential services. But he's also a man.

I checked my horniness barometer. Moderate. I picked up.

"I'm busy," I told him. "Go away." I stared out the windows at the cloudless blue sky. A perfect winter day, eighty degrees in the shade with a soft eastern breeze.

"Vanna, don't hang up. We got a problem, big problem. Guess who's on his way up?"

I didn't say anything. There was nothing I could say. The choices were multiple, and none would improve my day.

"You there?"

I was there, but I didn't want to be. I grunted, running a hand through my curls. They were wild today, making it a day like any other. Out of my control, basically.

"He just went up the back stairs, so you got maybe one minute to roll out. Jump on the elevator. Meet me in the lobby, and I'll buy you a drink. We'll hide out at the Tam."

Tempting, but I had another appointment later on. I wasn't in the mood to skip out on my work day. I wasn't worried about an unexpected visitor to the office, anyway.

"Chill out. I can handle it," I reassured my assistant and occasional fuck buddy.

He made one of those sounds, the clucking that indicates anxious disbelief. All too often, Ringo makes a fuss over nothing. A sensitive ex-cop on a NYPD pension and a permanent prescription for Effexor, Ringo takes everything to heart. Between the two of us, I'm known as the cool one. Which is really saying something since I'm, one, Irish; two, a flaming redhead; and three, female. But in our good cop/bad cop arrangement, Ringo's the softy. Not in the bedroom, though. But that's another story.

"I can take it. Hit me." I peered out the office door. The hall was empty, the elevators silent. "Who is it this time? Angry husband? Twisted lawyer? IRS?"

Ex-Treme Measures is publically marketed as a private investigation firm. We're registered as such with the state of Florida. Since we specialize in domestic relations investigations in an era in which everyone aspires to lead a television commercial life, we're constantly in demand. People in this part of the world seem to believe everything can be replaced, even though nothing can, not really. We make excellent money. We make excellent enemies. We get hassled and harassed. We threaten people, we testify in court. And, every once in a while, we get investigated ourselves.

To keep the Feds off our backs, we take on the normal cases—dirty divorces requiring surveillance evidence, abused wives seeking proof for restraining orders. We seek direct evidence including forensic data from home and business, financial reports, receipts, and phone bills. We check cars and beds for extramarital hair and body secretions, and we are not above digging through trash or swiping underwear. We handle the everyday cases as best we can, although photographing cheaters *en flagrante* or hard-asses slapping their women around can be a real downer. Fortunately, one out of every dozen of our cover cases results in a contract for our specialty services. This usually cheers the two of us up.

We're careful with our ex-treme cases, exceptionally careful. We leave no trail behind. So I wasn't particularly worried about being investigated. Any other surprise visitor I could handle as well. All part of the job description.

Ringo can really get his Joe Boxers in a wad, though. He doesn't like anyone in a cheap suit coming into our office and going through our files. Even though he knows I keep all the important data in my head. On the office computer and in the file cabinets—routine client forms, receipts for everyday services. The boys could look all they wanted. They wouldn't find anything to incriminate us.

Everyone else could kiss my ass.

While I waited for an answer to my question, I closed the door and collapsed on the red leather couch. Ringo was outside somewhere. I could hear the rush of wind through the phone. It sounded like he was on the run, breathing hard and whispering under his breath. It was nearly impossible for me to understand what he was telling me. I missed half of what he was saying, didn't get the rest. Typical male-female communication situation.

"You're gonna get a knock on the door any minute, Van. That asshat's on his way up. I was downstairs waitin' for Emworth. I'm tailin' her now. Then who should slither by—"

The tight fist knocking on the double oak panels of the office door spoke of an undeserved confidence and a phony strength. Maybe a little righteous anger, too. I knew that knock.

"Oh, shit," Ringo was saying as I hung up.

I had to agree. "Oh, shit," I said as I opened the door. "The hell you doing here?"

He brushed past me and dropped into one of the black leather wing chairs. He'd lost more weight since the last time I saw him, but his lanky form seemed to take up the entire room. Either the sun dipped behind a cloud or he'd brought one with him because suddenly the day darkened.

Ringo was right. I was not happy to see Ashton Treme. Not today, not any day. But I had no choice. I had to take a deep breath and sit down directly across from my not-yet-ex-husband and wait for an explanation for his unwelcome visit. One I was sure not to like.

He sneered and leered at me, accomplishing both at once, a feat perfected by men with an upper class background, no sense of propriety, and no class. He had pigeon feathers stuck in his greasy hair, bird shit on his scuffed shoes. I could smell the Opium from four feet away.

I pinched my nose. "You know how much I hate the smell of her perfume. Why do you keep coming here, Ashton? I'm busy."

"You don't look busy." His eyes skated around the edges of the room, taking in the floor-to-ceiling bookshelves, my massive rock on vinyl collection covering one wall, the video monitors and other equipment along a second wall, the double windows taking up most of the third. "Your desk hasn't a single paper on it. Methinks you sit here all day, wasting time and plotting your revenge."

My laugh sounded strained, even to my own ears. "Believe me, if I wanted revenge, I would have wreaked havoc on you seven years ago when I walked in on you. In *our* bed, with that *stupid* girl." I gave him a hard look. "All I want is for you to fuck off and stay fucked off, Ashton. You know that."

It was his turn to force a laugh. "But I can't, Vanna. Not when you and that Neanderthal are up to something. Something very lucrative." His voice rose. "I want in, Vanna. You know me, I want my share. So I'll hang around until you make me *want* to fuck off." He crossed one long leg over the other. His jeans hadn't been washed in ages. "You can make all this go away," he said, pointing to his scruffy face and grinning like a creepy Halloween pumpkin, "the usual way."

Ashton Treme was the only man alive who could bring my blood from a comfortable ninety-eight degrees—I run cool; my temperature's consistently below normal—up to the boiling point in mere seconds. The other men who were able to do that are dead. Deservedly so.

"I'd certainly *like* to make you go away." I gave him a heated stare.

His eyes bounced around, ball bearings on the loose. Obviously, his latest high was crashing. That was the sole reason for his visit.

"You're looking pretty primitive yourself, Ash," I said in a tightly controlled tone. I imagined standing over him with a hatchet, leaning in to give him a close haircut. "Ever hear of that popular mathematical formula, soap plus water? Or doesn't your little pussy tell you when you need to clean up your act? Maybe she's too dirtied up herself to notice."

He sat there staring at me, waiting for me to weaken. Give in.

He didn't care, but I couldn't stand hearing the catty weakness in my voice. His obvious indifference to my emotions was so insulting I stood up and turned my back on him. The image of bludgeoning my near-ex faded as I walked to the coatrack for my wallet. Sometimes, I hated myself, and this was one of those times. Getting rid of bad husbands was my trade. Why not Ashton Treme?

My heart was in the way on this one, and knowing that about myself depressed me. I liked to take action, and I'd been avoiding that with my almost-ex. I made up reasons to let him off the hook, excuses so lame I didn't fool anyone. Including myself.

I pulled my fat wallet out of the caramel-colored leather satchel that hung from a brass hook. Before I could turn around again, Ashton was up and across the room, embracing me from behind. He was on me like a heat rash on a runner's back.

"Baby, please don't give up on me. I'm working on getting clean, you know I am. Tammy's just a friend. A *using friend,* that's what they call Tammy in group."

A lot of good "group" had done him. He could quote their AA jargon as he sank deeper into his sorry-ass street life.

The whole time he was lying to me, his rotten breath in my ear, I tensed up. I tightened and tightened until my former husband was hugging a boulder, an unfeeling rock. The floral stink of cheap perfume mixed with the rank earth smell of his unwashed skin. I tried not to gag.

"If you can spare it, I need four hundred," my not-ex-soon-enough said. "To cover the room. Landlord thinks he's renting out suites at the Hyatt. Meanwhile, I got no hot water down the hall and the terlet hasn't been scrubbed since Bush was in office."

I chose this romantic moment to peel his fingers from my upper arms and slide free of his nauseating embrace. I held up my wallet, waving it between us like a white flag so he wouldn't attempt to reclaim me. Then I made for the desk and sat down at my computer. "I'm recording all the 'loans' I've been giving you, Ashton. One of these days, you'll be paying me back. With interest."

I meant when he inherited his family's fortune. He knew exactly what I meant.

While he hovered by the front door and watched, I counted out the bills I had on hand. Then I made a show of recording the amount on a spreadsheet on my computer. "You know, your timing's incredible. I'm actually flush today. Because I happened to stop at an ATM this morning, the one closest to the office. And that's exactly what happened the last time you dropped by for a 'loan.'"

I looked over. He had one bony hand in his mouth and was chewing on two fingers. Gnawing at himself, still staring at the money piled on my desk.

"Funny how you only show up on the days I stop at that bank on my way to work. Real coincidence, right, Ash?"

He didn't deny he'd been stalking me. Instead, he shrugged and continued to ogle the dough, transfixed. In an hour, the entire amount would be shit. Literally, because it would be up his ass. That's how the hardcore take their drugs now, "plugging" it right up the old a-hole. You shoot it up there with a bit of H2O and wait for the rapid response. Narcotics via rectum, the fastest way to get high.

Thinking about this made me want to take a hot shower as soon as possible.

"Three hundred twenty-four dollars. That's all I have. Unless you want a check?"

I flashed him a mean smile. Of course he didn't want a check. My to-be-ex, a former tax accountant and son of the owner of the biggest tax accounting firm in Palm Beach, had no bank account. He had no use for any financial institution. I almost felt sorry for Ashton and the addicts like him. People who threw away everything good in their lives in favor of plunging opiates up the ass. I could almost pity such people, but I'd watched too many times as my hard-earned money went to shit. So I felt something else. Disgust. Horror. Fear and loathing.

As I handed him the cash he was sure to waste, Ashton said with a sneer, "Thanks, babe. You're my hero."

"Are you still talking?" I asked. My way of reminding my husband it was time for him to leave.

He grabbed my hand and held on tight until I shook him off. I opened the office door and tilted my head in the *out* direction. I couldn't wait to go sterilize myself with huge squirts of antibacterial lotion.

Ashton paused in the doorway. "Tell Tarzan I'm on to him. Saw him downstairs, calling you to rat me out soon's I walked in the building."

He shook his head, as if he couldn't understand why I had such a person in my life. I said nothing, observing the most recent signs of his deterioration. He'd shaved off his shiny brown curls, his patchy buzz cut an additional detraction from his former good looks. His clean-cut, preppie, soccer goalie, Yale grad looks. Ashton Treme, a man who once dressed in Armani for work and pressed Izod for play. Did he even know how far he'd fallen?

"I don't know what you see in that big ape," my I-wish-he-were-ex-already said as he headed for the elevator. "Guy's a total loser."

Chapter Two

I was in the bathroom scrubbing my hands like a madwoman when Ringo popped his shiny head in. "Asshat gone? He looked like a baby turd, didn't he?"

We caught eyes in the mirror. My assistant didn't wait for a response. We both knew what he was up to. Ringo likes to point out the flaws in any man I might have feelings for. An easy job, I must admit. The ones who aren't dead are full of holes. So are some of the dead ones.

"Used to be able to fool everyone, had that snooty way about him." He furrowed his thick black brows, his dark eyes warning me to listen. "Not anymore. What a fuckstick. Man's a walking billboard for Just Say No. He's FTD, that one."

Fixin' to die was what my assistant meant. I knew what he meant, but I didn't want to hear it.

Drying my hands on a peach colored towel, I said, "So? Can we talk about work, please?" The rude way I said it, my assistant had to know I meant business. "Tell me the update."

I blobbed antibacterial goop on the center of one palm and rubbed my hands together. I was trying not to picture where my ex's fingers had been. This wasn't working. My mind kept flashing up images I really didn't want to see.

"Tell me where Mrs. Emworth went after she left

here," I ordered.

My assistant continued to stare down at me. I'm tall for a woman, but Ringo towers over me. And he's double my weight, all muscle. "How much he hit you up for this time?"

I hated it when my assistant ignored what I said in favor of grilling me on something I wasn't in the mood to discuss. I shook my head. My hands felt sticky and strange, like they were still contaminated. I wiped them on the towel, then sniffed them carefully. The palms smelled like a hospital room, sterile, bleached. But they probably wouldn't feel clean for the rest of the day, no matter what I did.

"He'll never step it up. And I'm sick of him coming here, sponging off you. Why don't you let me take that asshole down, Van?"

Asshole. Did he have to use that word?

Ringo sniffed. He knew I wouldn't give him the go-ahead, but he persisted in discussing his views on the topic. Even when I asked him to let it go. "Any day now, he's gonna go vox. Get fucken violent on you. I don't see why we can't put that dirty mutt out of his misery. Get him off your back. And ours."

I needed to get myself out of the powder room, where Ringo and his opinions were overwhelming me. When I pushed on his wide chest, he stepped back to let me pass. He smelled like peppermint toothpaste and sporty sweat. Yum.

"Hey, face facts, Van. The guy's got a death wish anyway. FTD, with all the shit he's been doin'. Right? So why don't we just move up the deadline for him? Do the world a fucken favor? Clean up the streets of Deport Beach, and all that?"

I would've liked to agree with my partner but, in all honesty, I couldn't. I could've lied and said my reasons were purely financial, but the truth was I had a slim, naïve, basically retarded hope Ashton Treme would undergo a miraculous transformation and return to his former self. During the ten years we were together, only the last six months were bad. Before that, I'd been crazy about him and he'd been wild about me.

Then, overnight, he morphed from a reliable, suave, successful tax professional to an untrustworthy cheat, a sniveling liar, and a degenerate addict. He'd gone from someone who cared for me to a user with a bad case of acquired narcissism. The change had been so dramatic, so shocking, my mind had yet to catch up. A part of me hung on to the former incarnation of my husband, stubbornly refusing to admit *that* man was gone.

That part of me made the rest of me sick. I'd been struggling with myself over the whole thing for way too long. It was exhausting. Ashton had devolved into one of those people you smell on the sidewalk as you pass by, a cardboard hut dweller, a pathetic bum, a bullying mooch. I'd let him ruin my life for too long before I recovered my senses and manned up. Now he just ruined my day. And not every day, either. Mainly when he was desperate for a handout. Still, why didn't I just go ahead and ex-terminate the motherfucker? He was the ultimate bad husband, so why was I at all hesitant to buck up and get it over with?

Who knows, but now was not the time for deep analysis of my sick romanticism. I grabbed my assistant's meaty arm right below the blood-red heart tattoo.

"Are you still talking?" I warned. "Like I've explained to you a million freaking times, we need to wait until he inherits the company. If we take him out now, his father will rewrite the trust and I'll be left out. As it is, I'll only win on a technicality. The whole family knows we're separated. And they all hate me now. They like to blame me for Ash's rapid decline."

"I know, I know," Ringo muttered. "But he's such a punk. I wish you'd at least let me hang his scrawny ass out to dry. It just pisses me off to see him come sniffin' around, dirty paw out…"

Scrawny ass. Dirty paw. I swallowed the bile that had crept up my throat and forced a smile.

We stood close together, absorbing one another's body heat. Ringo was instinctual in his desire to protect me. Like a giant Rottweiler. I patted my assistant on his hard chest. It was like slapping a redwood trunk. My horniness barometer bumped up a notch. He had such a big heart, a big everything. His pumped up body made my knees weak. He took my hand, stroking my wrist with his thumb. Softly, just enough to remind me how much I liked his touch.

After a tender moment, I withdrew my hand and moved away. As I stepped around him, I reminded us both why today was not a good day for a quickie between clients. "Let's go through the Emworth case, Ring. Then I've got Mrs. Cantor at three. After that, I might take you up on that drink."

Ringo's boyish face lit up. He knew exactly where having a drink would lead, because it always did. I like to think it's the wild Irish in me that makes me a cheap date, a fast drunk, and a reliable lay.

With some amusement, I watched him sneak a

peek at the grandfather clock next to the coatrack. He rubbed his big hands together like he was ready to chow down. On me. His grin was wide enough that I caught the flash of two gold molars. Then he used his best PI voice to give me the update. Finally. "After leaving the building, Mrs. Emworth climbed into her limo. Her ass may have been surgically enhanced, I'm not sure, but I did my best to survey the terrain."

Typical male joke. I didn't respond. I try not to encourage them, but it's impossible, really. I waved my hand as if to say, go on.

"I followed them to Atlantic Ave., then east to the Intracoastal. Jojo, her driver, dropped her in front of Café Bouchard, where she met up with two females. Older ladies, dressed expensively, lots of bling, body plastic. Definitely not cops. They sat at a table near the fountain, ordered cosmopolitans. Jojo and I had a little talk, and he agreed to represent. Now my man's got me on speed dial."

I nodded. "You did all that in like ten minutes? Impressive. So, okay. We'll let her go for now. She seems like a straight shooter, knows what she wants, willing to pay to get it done." I showed him the check, flapped it like a fan. "Bet you fifty she calls in the hit before the week's out."

He shook his head. "I'm not gonna lose another Grant to you, not this week. I need to hold onto my money. Saving up for a trip to Auckland with my hot girlfriend."

Ringo would make a great boyfriend. He likes to take me places, pay for things. He gets off on making plans. Another aspect of his irresistible charm. He'd been hinting about us going to a distant island for several months, but I was resisting. Business had become tricky lately, and I felt a need to stay put. Key West was a maybe, New Zealand was totally out.

"Fine, be that way," I said with a shrug. "Keep your dough, loser boy. We both know I'll be one hundred percent right, as usual." I grinned.

When I checked my buzzing phone, I had a text from the vet's. Porsche and Popeye were done with their tune-up. "So, what's the latest on Mrs. Cantor?" I asked my assistant.

Ringo snorted. "That one's a real headcase. A fifty-one/fifty."

Cop talk for insane. He swirled his finger by his ear to indicate how crazy he thought she was.

I wasn't so sure. I figured she was playing the nut role on purpose. Women sometimes act loony to get the cheating man's attention. It never works, not in the long run. Being out of your mind just gives your guy more reason to ditch you.

Ringo dropped his bulk onto the couch, which creaked in protest, and pulled out his pocket notebook. After flipping through the wrinkled pages, he stopped to read from his notes. A flock of parrots squawked by overhead, drowning out the first few words.

"—Bethesda Hospital psyche ward. She was released after forty-eight hours." He looked up. "My man tells me they gave her a good butt-shot of Thorazine when she came in. Stabilized her. Did some tests, interviews with the shrink on call. Gave her a prescript and sent her back out on the streets." He shook his head. "I'm kinda scared of that one. She might cut my nuts off, she has the chance. She's a real man-hater." He shivered.

24

"That's where you're wrong. Bella Cantor works in a garage, for god's sake. Sitting at the front desk like she does all day? She's got to answer to all the customers, mostly men in love with their cars. She works with a half-dozen mechanics as well as the owner, that good old boy from Okeechobee. No man-hater would last at a job like that."

Ringo had seen her in action with the guys in the shop. She juggled them like greased Superballs. Why didn't he get it? Bella didn't hate all men. Just the one who deserved it.

"Believe me, she's just angry," I added. "And she has every right to be."

"What about slicing into her husband the way she claims she did? Using a kitchen knife to trim his balls? You call that man-love?" He covered his crotch with his hands. "Van, come on. You really think she's just a sweet li'l gal whose man done her wrong?"

Bella wasn't a rich bitch from Palm Beach. She had a tough life, and she had a lot more guts than most of my clients did.

I smiled. "No, I'd never call Bella sweet. Or little. But she's not a killer. And she's not crazy. She's just got an active case of TI."

TI is what we call the period of instability many of our clients experience upon discovering their mate has been unfaithful and plans to leave them. TI stands for temporary insanity. It's one hundred percent normal for jilted women to go through this stage of emotional upheaval when their man goes rogue. Some recover quickly before they hurt anyone. Others…well, we've all read stories about men waking up to a sudden onset of matrimonial castration. TI can get ugly, real ugly.

"Maybe," Ringo said, "but I ain't stickin' around to find out. That scary bitch gives me the willies."

We agreed to meet at the Tam at four-thirty. Before the door shut behind him, my assistant answered his phone with a hearty, "Jojo, my man. What you got for me?"

He gave me a cute little wave. I smiled and waved back.

Later for you, big boy, was what I was thinking. I didn't need to check my horniness barometer. *Down, girl,* was what I told myself. And then I thought, *Are you still talking?*

****

I pulled up Mrs. Cantor's file and printed out her structured payment sheet. Unlike Mrs. Emworth, Bella was on an installment plan and I billed her using a sliding scale. She couldn't afford us otherwise, but she really needed our help. Her marriage had gone bad, and she'd hired us for the usual domestic surveillance, hoping we could provide evidence her husband was cheating. I wasn't sure if she knew about the ex-tra measures we offered, but I was ready to turn her down if she requested our special services. Mrs. Cantor's case was nothing more than a normal domestic investigation, just your everyday suspicious spouse.

Her suspicions were about to be confirmed.

She arrived on time, and we settled on the couch together. Her black hair hung limp around her pasty face. She looked exhausted, her red-rimmed eyes vague and clouded. The decline and fall of yet another American female due to matrimonial disputes. It was disheartening.

When I offered her a cup of coffee, she burst into

tears. I took that as a yes and passed her a box of tissues before I made my way across the room to the kitchenette.

"I know what you're going to tell me," she mumbled between wet breaths. "You've got photos of him with a younger woman."

"No, I do not." I wasn't lying, either. "Sugar?" I asked over the hiss and grumble of my One Touch espresso maker.

She nodded, dabbing at her soft brown eyes with a wad of the tissue. "Yes, please. But what are you saying? No girlfriend? How can that be? He hasn't laid a hand on me in almost two years." When she dropped her head, her double chins sagged in a most unattractive way. Tears coursed down her plump cheeks. "Do you think I need to lose weight?"

They all ask that, even the model-thin trophy wives. When men cheat, women automatically assume we're to blame. We invariably think it must be due to our own lack of attractiveness. We worry it's our fault when a man strays. Usually, it's not. Take a look at evolutionary biology. The animal world illustrates only too clearly this dire fact—most species are not monogamous. This uncomfortable and unromantic truth has nothing to do with excess adipose and everything to do with survival of the species. Male animals, including our human partners, are hard-wired to fuck around, making sure their genetic material gets passed along to the next generation. Simple as that.

But I didn't go into all that with my client. Even though her case was different and there were some unusual factors contributing to the domestic impasse, I knew how she felt. All she wanted to hear was what she could do to fix the situation. Like all betrayed women, Bella was looking for a solution to her domestic problem.

No matter what the socioeconomic class, level of education, age, or situation in life, all my clients want the same things. First they want me to tell them there's a simple fix. They want to learn there's a diet, an exercise regimen, a new coital position that will make their stray decide to stay. Unfortunately, life is not that benevolent. Once they learn that, depression sets in.

For some, the hollow sadness evolves into anger. They seek ex-treme measures. These women want me to make the problem go away. Permanently.

Sometimes, I'm able to assist. But not all the time.

I added a handful of sugar substitute packets to a silver serving tray, piling them beside a small pitcher of cream and two sterling demitasse cups. While I poured us each a shot of steaming coffee, I said to my client, "There's a manila folder on the table in front of you. Please take a look at the photos my assistant took last week."

This was the absolute worst part of my job. Worse than ex-terminating bad husbands and way more painful. It's not easy for me to pop a cheater and toss him in the deep blue sea. But it's excruciating to show his wife explicit photos of him in action. Because, as horrible as it can be to walk in on your husband while he's in the throes of passion with someone young enough to be your daughter—and believe me, that hurts like a steak knife to the gut—it can be even more traumatic to come face to face with the cold hard evidence that the man you love's been doing you wrong by doing somebody else. Photos of your man, naked and ecstatic in the arms of that someone else? This is enough to push some women over the brink of despair.

Bella Cantor, for one, had already tumbled down the other side of desperate. She'd considered cutting off his balls, but she'd chickened out when he woke up screaming. Fortunately for everyone concerned, she let go and he quickly moved out. After that, she stalked him, threatened him, and threw either herself or heavy objects at him. He said he needed space. He was afraid of her rage. He wanted time to think. And, like most guilty husbands, he kept insisting there was no other woman in his life.

They all say that. When Bella came to us in tears, Ringo spent two weeks tailing her husband. The evidence was clear. Steven Cantor was telling the truth.

Before I could set the tray down on the glass coffee table, my client burst into hysterical laughter. This morphed into hysterical weeping, yet somehow she was laughing at the same time. Falling apart in all the usual ways, her lurching emotions the perfect match for the absurdity of the situation.

Discovering your hunch was correct and your spouse has indeed betrayed you brings on a medley of reactions from shock to catatonia. Discovering your husband has betrayed you for a man, or men, elicits an array of additional responses that can range from relief to disbelief to outright hysteria.

"One fake sugar or two?" I asked Mrs. Cantor.

She gagged, then giggled. Her eyes were rolling around in her head. The woman needed medication, a therapist, nurturing. I'd start with the coffee, then move on to a referral.

"If you want, I can stir in the sugar for you while

the coffee's still piping hot."

My clients usually find this kind of distraction calming. It helps them to switch focus, to think about how *they* like things, how *they* have a say, how *they* can control what happens to them. One sugar, two? *I want Sweet 'n' Low* or *Do you have agave?* The little things help when you've been overswept by a tidal wave of wild emotions.

"Two, please," she managed to tell me between fits. "Oh, my god, I had no *idea*. I had *no* idea!"

I handed her the cup, which required her to sit up straight and stop writhing all over the couch. She sipped her coffee while I retrieved the black and white, eight-by eleven-inch photos from her lap. I held them up, showing her the live action shots one at a time—Steven in the parking lot of his office building at night, deep in lip-lock with a young male; Steven and another hot young thing in skinny jeans, walking hand in hand into a triple-X movie theatre; Steven and a middle-aged man, both shirtless, drinking martinis at an outdoor bar; a blurry window shot of two male bodies pretzeled together on a tousled bed, Steven recognizable due to the distinctive white streaks in his jet black hair.

"This explains everything," my client said, finally calming. "I always thought he lacked a normal sex drive. I had to initiate, and sometimes he lost interest before we'd even gotten started." She looked at me, her round face red with embarrassment. "The way he treats me, like I mean nothing to him. He gives me no money, makes me work that crappy receptionist job to support myself. Meanwhile, he's rolling in it. Like anyone would be who owns a chain of Laundro-bars."

I didn't want to point out that Steven was possibly

the *only* person who owned a chain of Laundromats that also served as singles bars. So I sipped my coffee and let her talk. After the reveal, the client always needs to air her thoughts, to sift through her memories and explore her own psyche. Had she known he was gay but hadn't dared admit it to herself? Was she no longer responsible for his betrayal, and could she therefore forgive him for it?

As she wondered about these things out loud, going through the normal sorting out process, I offered an array of sounds to underline my agreement, encouragement, or support. This aspect of my job was more therapy than anything else. She'd move on from me to her family, her closest girlfriends, her rabbi. I would recommend a psychiatric social worker who was familiar with this kind of domestic situation. Loss can be liberating as well as disconcerting. Hopefully, Bella could adjust to the reality of her marriage and, with it behind her, move on with her own life.

I checked the clock, wondering if I might just let her go. Did we really need to burden this client with a long-term payment plan for services rendered? Her husband was playing cheap with her, and now he'd dealt her the ultimate rip-off card. Why add to the poor woman's suffering? I was about to tell her this when Mrs. Cantor leaned forward and dropped the bomb.

"I guess I don't want to kill him," she said, instantly capturing my undivided attention.

She knows about our special services.

"He can't help who he is," she added.

The voice of reason. *That was fast*, I wanted to say. Most wives take at least a few weeks to come to their senses and face the rational conclusion there's nothing to be done.

But the bomb she'd just lobbed exploded in my face.

"Guess I'll have to call off the hitman," she said.

The hitman?

My heart chilled itself to a slow pump as I waited for my lungs to start up again. When I knew I could speak without stuttering, I said, "I hope you're joking, Mrs. Cantor. If you're not, I will be forced to report this conversation to the proper authorities."

Meaning, I was going to run straight to Ringo. We couldn't be linked to an intended homicide. It would be bad for business. Homicide *is* our business, yes, but subtle, carefully planned, untraceable homicide. Knowing Mrs. Cantor's financial situation, I figured her hit had probably been arranged via Craigslist. Or she'd hired a low-IQ dropout, a troubled teenager who spent his time selling nickel bags behind the local fast-food joint.

Mrs. Cantor set down her empty cup. "Don't worry. I can call him right now and tell him there's been a change of plans."

Before I could stop her, she whipped out her cell and pressed the shortcut key. Wow. I wondered if I had been programmed in the top spot for any of my clients. I'm sorry to say this, but a powerful wave of jealousy passed through me like a bad Mexican dinner.

"Mrs. Cantor, you can't make that call here—"

Too late. He'd answered on the first ring. Whoa. I was on top of it for my clients, but this was exceedingly impressive service. I wanted to grab the phone and press speaker. Instead, I listened carefully to her side of the conversation and planned what I would say when she hung up.

"My husband is gay." Mrs. Cantor sounded proud and defensive. *See? Not my fault he's leaving.* "I've decided to terminate our arrangement. I'll need a refund."

As she listened to the response, her face crumpled. She looked at me, fat tears streaming over the hills of her pale cheeks. I knew exactly what her hired gun was saying. *No money back, lady. Tough shit.*

Most people in the hit business will not return your deposit. Some will come after you, trying for the whole enchilada, blackmailing you with the threat of exposure unless you pay the full tab for a job never completed. Some keep milking you, sometimes for years afterward. They've got serious leverage over you, and the worst of them won't hesitate to use it.

There's a special place in hell for people like that.

My body temperature heated up a little, enough so that I could feel beads of sweat dotting my forehead. The heat itself felt predatory. I wanted to kill someone. Someone bad.

Mrs. Cantor choked on her tears and clicked off.

"What did he say?" I asked.

I couldn't help myself. She was the color of a whitewall tire. Her body sagged off the couch, slumped and airless. Like a whitewall tire that's gone flat.

"He said it's too late. Steve's already dead."

Oh, shit. Now I felt like crying myself. Steven Cantor was a public figure in certain circles. The local news would cover the story. There would be a small furor over the demise of the local owner of a chain of swinging laundromats. People would talk. It seemed all too likely a police investigation would be launched.

And we'd be in for some shit throwing. As the investigation firm hired by the deranged wife, the one who'd threatened to cut off her husband's balls, Ex-Treme Measures would look bad. Our discrete image would be sullied.

My heart raced, but I kept my voice calm as I tended to the client. I let her cry it out, replenishing her coffee, murmuring words of comfort. At some point, however, I allowed my own emotions to get the better of me and blurted, "This situation calls for Ex-Treme Measures."

Bella sat up and looked me in the eye. She nodded her head in agreement and stopped crying.

"Thank you," she said. "I trust you. I know you can help me."

Even though I smiled at that, I had no idea what we could do to help. But I knew we had to do something about my client's trigger-happy hitman. What an amateur. You don't kill off the gay spouse in a troubled marriage. There was no point to it. Had this person even conducted an investigation? I doubted it. He'd wanted the payoff so he took out the mark. What a slob.

After Mrs. Cantor left, I called Ringo. I held off on explaining the situation to him, but I couldn't help thinking about how unprofessional the hitman had been in what was obviously a very delicate situation. He'd need to be addressed and, possibly, redressed. As a dead man.

My blood heated to such a roiling boil that perspiration coursed between my breasts. I think it was Aristotle who taught his followers the sole purpose of the brain was to cool down the blood. He claimed it was the mind that "tempers the heat and seething of the heart." Something like that. In my case, it seemed to be my brain that directly ignited my bloodstream. But maybe it was just my Irish heart.

If my assistant had been able to press his big shiny head against my heaving chest right then, he might have heard a simmering sound. As it was, he said, "I'll try and nab us a booth."

I grabbed my leather bag and closed up shop for the day.

Chapter Three

The Tam was packed, as usual, and thrumming with the full sound of low-pitch conversation. It's so recognizable, the distinct hum of discussions between drunk rich people. They create a specific decibel, the one percenters, especially when they're stoked on top-shelf booze. It must be because they feel like they deserve all the airtime they can get, so they let the swell of their self-inflated voices fill up the room. Sometimes this sucks out all the fresh air, sharpening the sound. If you've got more than a handful of these folks in a crowded space, I swear, the din can crush your lungs.

We sat in the middle of the room at a small table for two. No booths available. The crowd surged around us. Prada, Dior, Versace, Armani. The flash of gold bling, diamond chunks, weighty gemstones, capped teeth. The music pulsed, Frank Sinatra alternating with Adele. The men were mostly middle-aged or older, the women under fifty and hungry.

We were out of place, but then again, we usually are. Ringo and I frequent the Tam in order to troll for clients. And to get a buzz on. Our version of foreplay.

"I have to pick up my babies before six," I warned Ringo as he slid a draft beer my way. A very full pint of a very black beer. "Dr. T closes up at six on the dot."

He grinned. "Try this, Van. Espresso Stout. I'm tellin' you, you'll love it. It wakes you up while it mellows you out. Superior combo. Three for one until six, so I already had a pint before you got here and it's fucken awesome. Chill." He tucked the cold glass in my outstretched hand. "Listen to me, I'm a goddamn connoisseur. It's good shit, man."

My preferences ran to name brand beer in bottles, which was why my assistant was giving me the hard sell. But I shrugged, "Sounds perfect." I took a deep whiff. The head had foamed into a creamy froth that smelled like coffee beans. "Whoa."

Ringo laughed. I had to trust my assistant on this one. When it came to mind-altering beverages, he knew what he was talking about. He'd turned me on to some fantastic microbrewery beers, truly excellent red wines from Chile and Argentina, and the best drug and alcohol combos for knocking out a mark. So, what could I do? I drank up.

Shit *was* good. I licked the foam from my upper lip and grinned. I swigged more beer and listened to the men in the booth behind us bragging about their portfolios. If one of them mentioned a mistress, I could get interested.

"There should be rules," Ringo said, ending my eavesdropping. "No polo club assholes allowed in Irish bars. Right? The loopholers and the taxpayer's dime crowd will not be served here."

"Don't be ridiculous. We wouldn't come here looking for clients if they banned all the big phonies. We need these snobs. Our bread and caviar, right?"

Ringo frowned. When I downed the rest of my pint in one long gulp, my assistant leaned forward. His thick pink lips were slick with cocoa colored foam. I wanted to lick it off. I already had a decent buzz, and suddenly

I wanted more.

"S'up, Van? You're drinking like you're in Dublin." His frown deepened. "It's that bastard ex of yours, isn't it? He upset you today." Ringo leaned farther across the marble-topped table between us, his impressive biceps bulging from under his tight white T-shirt. "I'm gonna have to beat that guy's nasty ass, no matter what you say."

Nasty ass. I swallowed hard. Some beer lurched back up my esophagus, so I swallowed again and shook my head. "This is not about Ashton. We got worse shit to take care of." I held up my empty. "Get me another one of these suckers, and we'll discuss."

My assistant did as he was told. That was the best thing about sleeping with a man on an irregular, unpredictable basis. He would do anything to sleep with you again. Including refilling your drink order. Especially refilling your drink order.

Over a second round of ES, my new favorite drink, I told Ringo about Bella and Steven Cantor's unfortunate business arrangement. I kept my voice real low. Not that the Tam clientele cared to listen. The second best thing about our favorite bar—the Prada crowd has no interest in other people's business. They're way too wrapped up in their own.

Ringo shrugged and sipped his beer. "So? We find out who this joker is, where he hangs. If he's local, I eliminate the competition. He don't know we exist, but we know all about him. *Art of War*—prepare to meet the enemy. I'll handle this. No problem."

My thirst had eased up, fortunately, so I was able to consider Ringo's viewpoint on the issue with a somewhat clear head. Three beers, and I'd be three sheets. More, and they'd be scraping me off the walls. Vanna Treme does her Jackson Pollock impersonation. Again.

It was my turn to shrug. "Easy to say, but I don't think so. Cuz I doubt it'll be so simple. Here's the thing. She hired this guy over the Internet. Never met him, has nothing but a phone number and a name. Mr. Grey."

"As in, *Fifty Shades of*?" Ringo's mind was headed down the single track men all jumped on after a drink or two. Already he'd undressed me in his mind and was licking his way up from my bare toes. I could almost feel his sandpapery tongue swirling around my right ankle bone.

When I shivered, he laughed. He knew exactly what I was thinking he was thinking. Because he was. Thinking it, I mean.

I gave him the look. The one that said, *Okay, have it your way with me. But let me have a few drinks first.*

Ringo's dark eyes glittered. "Gimme that contact info. I'll take care of Grey. You've got enough to deal with right now. Fucking Ashton, for one." He paused, thinking. "You should focus on the clients who actually pay us, unlike Mrs. Cantor. You didn't even charge her the full fee, did you?" He didn't bother to wait for an answer. "Shit, Van. Are we a nonprofit organization?" He sighed, sipped his dark beer. Then he brightened a little. "Although Mrs. Emworth's good for it. That one's an ace."

He settled back against the slatted rungs of the chair. His shoulders were as puffed up as a couple of down pillows. I wanted to lay my head down on one and float off to a dreamless sleep. That would never happen, though. My sleep is conducted in private, and it's rarely dreamless. For me, sleep itself is all too rare. I'm a terrible sleeper.

"Jojo called from Town Center where Mrs. Emworth was rackin' up a huge bill, all charged up on vodka and hen talk. Right before you got here, the kid checked in again. The boss was at home. Alone. He says she hurried upstairs, buzzed and all loaded down with half a dozen shopping bags. From the Secret, mainly."

I nodded. The new client was following my directions, even if she knew how hopeless it was. That was one retainer I would've really enjoyed returning. Why couldn't love overcome all, maybe just once in a while?

Sometimes the need for my services makes me sad. Why are men and women so mismatched? Our bodies were designed for love. We ooze hormones when we have sex, gushing neurochemicals that make us feel something special for our partners. Humans are drawn to coupling, forming pairs bonded for both sexual and social reasons, and our culture endorses this arrangement. Yet, the male tends to lose interest. He is extremely likely to wander. Knowing this is true throughout the animal kingdom doesn't make it any easier to accept.

Sometimes I wish my business would become obsolete, with no need for Ringo and me to do what we've learned to do best.

Drinking and thinking always form an unhappy coupling. I took a deep breath and centered myself. Then I took a deeper swig of the bitter beer. My job was to help my clients, not mourn their failed romances. Plus, I was off duty.

"You'd look great in something from the Secret," my assistant said. "Something firehouse red. Made out of see-through silk, short and sweet. And maybe edible." He licked his wet lips. "Definitely edible."

We stared at one another. My assistant's charcoal eyes smoldered.

I sighed. I knew enough about men to say, "Fine. Let's go pick up my babies. We can talk about our business crises later."

His joy was childlike, and I loved him for that. But only for the night. I love my men one at a time, but never forever. I advise all my clients to do the same.

Nobody ever listens to me on this.

****

Dusk had come and gone, ushering in a refreshing coolness. I rolled down all the windows in my rusty VW and allowed the night air to slap me around. Ringo followed me in his SUV, a manly black on black Escalade, as I drove—slowly, careful as a drunk landlord—all the way up Federal Highway to Trainor's Veterinary Clinic. I parked near the front door and hurried inside. My assistant stayed in the empty lot with his gas-guzzling motor running.

"Dr. T, how's life?" I asked the small brown man in green scrubs hovering behind the reception desk. His receptionist had already left for the day. And the waiting room lights were off. I felt like a shit, holding the man up while I hit happy hour with my pal. "Sorry I'm late."

He gave me the once over and, I'm sure, drew the obvious conclusion. Half-drunk. Which half? That was the question in all men's minds when they saw a woman in my giddy condition.

"Your kids are in perfect health," Dr. T reported. "But you're right when you say they don't seem to be bonding. Have you noticed the male's begun exhibiting some feather plucking behavior? Stress related."

I nodded. "Suggestions?" I didn't want my beautiful boy to pick at himself. "Is any relationship worth such self-destruction?" I wondered aloud.

Dr. Trainor laughed. "Birds tend to be better in a relationship. Happier, more content. This is because birds are more monogamous than most animals. Including humans," he said with a wink. My vet was a font of information on evolutionary biology. He was always up on the latest research in animal behavior. "Your birds are the right age for breeding. For many species, the male bird is heavily involved in the parenting, helping to build the nest, sitting on eggs, feeding offspring. So periods of monogamy do occur in the wild. It's in the avian genes, their nature. In captivity, without other options, I would imagine your parrots will eventually pair up."

He smiled at me so I gave him a lopsided smile in return. Dr. Trainor knows I have issues with some of his views on pair bonding. But I do like to hear his opinions on the subject. Learning about the latest research on animal behavior from an expert helps me when I'm facing a distraught client who wants to put an end to her suffering. *No biggie. If this were a pair of black vultures, the flock would simply peck the philanderer to death.*

Of course, Dr. Trainor has no idea about the special services offered by Ex-Treme Measures. Since he believes long-term monogamy is unnatural because it is so rare in the animal world, he would never approve of certain aspects of my business. In fact, if he knew some of my more ex-treme policies, he would probably tell me I'm fighting a losing battle against human nature itself.

We settled the bill, and I waited outside the double doors while Dr. Trainor went into the back rooms to retrieve my birds. When he returned, two large cardboard travel carriers in hand, I blurted, "Dr. T, what about female birds? Do they ever go outside the pair bond?"

He handed me the disposable carriers. My poor babies flapped their wings nervously, bumping against the sides of the padded boxes. I couldn't see them fidgeting, but I could feel their angst. They didn't like to be enclosed. Trapped, and in the dark. Who could blame them?

My vet folded his arms across his chest. "Both sexes will have extra-pair copulations if they have the option. DNA tests on offspring show that females regularly lay eggs fertilized by males other than their mate. And males mate with females outside the pair bond, even going beyond their own clan, so to speak, in search of sexual variety. There are good, solid, evolutionary reasons for this behavior."

I glanced down at his plain gold wedding ring. I wondered if Mrs. Trainor would one day seek my services. I didn't want that to happen. He was a smart man and a terrific vet.

"Sexual desire for multiple partners is biological, and it exists to ensure a species evolves. More diverse genes, better chances for rapid species evolution. This is true with birds as well as people." He walked me to the door. I had a good ten inches on him, even in flats. "Females will mix it up, but it is the male biology that bodes ill for monogamy, I'm afraid. Male animals actually produce more sperm during extra-pair copulations than in sexual acts with a mate. Think about the sociobiological implications of that fact alone."

Out in the lot, Ringo was still waiting, engine purring in the quiet night. My car sat between the lines, crooked in the parking space. Like an old lady, a half-blind old lady from mainland China, had parked it there.

I ignored my embarrassment, because I was thinking about the women who came to me in tears, devastated by their fear of abandonment, ruined by their broken lives, their shattered hearts. How could that be a natural process? How would these women use such overwhelming loss to achieve any kind of self-evolution? I couldn't see it happening, not with the clients I'd been serving.

My vet kept talking about the science, leaving out the emotions involved. "Males' sexual behavior is geared toward quantity of offspring while the female's behavior ensures quality. This is a cross-species trait. What this says for social mores may be difficult to accept. When the discussion turns to divorce, I'm not the most popular person at a dinner party." He opened the tinted glass doors for me. "I don't like to pretend that whatever a culture chooses to endorse is what's best for the individuals living within it. I think you and I are agreed on this."

"Oh yeah," I said. "But I'm not sure we agree about the value of monogamy to the individual." My birds shifted, and one of them squawked. I needed to get them home and out of their padded cell. "According to Freud, civilization itself is based on the repression of natural instincts. So, in my mind, monogamy is a healthy, learned trait. A positive, educated choice. I mean, what's natural may not always be what's best for us. If evolving depends on us being civilized, that is."

I think I said *shivilished*. Time to head home before I embarrassed myself any further.

Dr. Trainor didn't seem to notice. He just nodded, his handsome face serious. He appeared to be ignoring my inebriation. I wondered if any of his other patients would listen to all the data he liked to share. Knowing Palm Beach and its uptight denizens, I had to figure I was one of his only confidants. "True, Vanna. But we're not seeking to excuse bad behavior, you and I. We're trying to understand it."

I had to agree with that.

Chapter Four

I hustled the bird carriers up the walk and onto the front porch, setting them down on the newspaper I used to protect the Mexican tile. Ringo followed us in and locked the screen door behind us. I slipped out of my Merrells. The tile felt cool on my bare feet.

Before I could let her out, my female parrot began to protest. "Yo mutha. Bros befo' hos."

Ringo laughed. "Now, Porsche," he said to the outside of the box holding the female African Grey. "None of that nasty rap talk. What'll your boyfriend think?"

"He won't tell us what he thinks, will you, Popeye?" I cooed as I opened the other box and reached in for my male African Grey. "Come to mama."

"Fuckin' ho, fuckin' ho," Porsche screeched.

We laughed, but I could just imagine my neighbors, frowning and slamming their windows. Over the years, several had filed complaints with the city. People just do not like parrot talk, especially dirty parrot talk. Fortunately, I had a few contacts on the Deport Beach force. And I wasn't breaking any laws. Unlike a lot of people living in South Florida, I'd chosen a *legal* non-native animal for a pet. Not some wild animal stolen from a rainforest in South America or Africa or somewhere.

I'd purchased Popeye as a baby from a parrot

breeder in Margate. I brought him home when he was only four months old. He bonded instantly and adored me like a lover. But, as he matured, the mismatch became obvious. I knew my parrot needed to attach himself to a winged female. He was spending most of his day alone. I didn't want my cutie pie to be lonely and depressed. I was worried Popeye would pluck out his lovely silver-gray feathers if he felt abandoned.

In retrospect, Popeye had been fine on his own. Now that Porsche shared his living space, my boy was indulging in feather destructive behavior. Go figure.

"Poor Popeye," Ringo said. "He don't dare speak. Not anymore. Porsche scares the shit out of him."

As if on cue, Popeye crapped, grazing the edge of my hand. Yellow goo dripped onto my foot, splattering my ankle and painting my toes an unattractive hue. Ringo would have to begin his ardent lovemaking at another spot on my torso if he knew what was good for him.

"Maybe he annoys her and that's why she screams," I said as I cuddled my bright-eyed love to my chest. He nibbled at the loose threads around the buttons on my oxford-style shirt. "Are you a big pain in the arse, Popeye? Can't you clean up your act enough to please your pretty young girlfriend?"

He said nothing, pecking gently around my breasts. It looks strange when he does that, but when you think about it, he's only fourteen. A curious teenage boy.

Porsche screeched loud enough that Ringo jammed his fingers in his ears and backed away. She was cranky and she had a potty mouth, but Porsche wasn't a biter. Popeye, on the other hand, was fiercely protective of me and often snapped at male visitors. He'd ripped into

Ashton a number of times and drawn blood more than once from Ringo. In fact, there are a number of men with beak-shaped scars walking around Deport Beach. And elsewhere, to be honest. I haven't been nearly as discriminating as I should. One of my numerous personality flaws.

As soon as I set him on his stand, Popeye began preening himself.

"Why don't you let your girlfriend do that?" I said for the millionth time.

The bird ignored me, as usual, so I crouched down to remove Porsche from the carrier.

"Fuck off," she said in her gravelly pimp voice.

Ringo laughed. We'd inherited Porsche from one of our clients, the wife of a small time marijuana peddler named Cochraine. Ringo liked the bird more than I did, but he wasn't about to bring her home to his meticulous, minimalist bachelor pad on the beach.

"No, no, no," she yelled in a high pitched voice as I lifted her to her stand. "Nooooooo."

"The uniforms will be here any minute," Ringo said, glancing at his diver's watch. "It's lucky they know I'm not some messed up manhandler, or I might get charged with something."

"Hey, they've rushed cruisers to the scene of supposed domestic abuse when I've been here all alone. Most of those guys are familiar now with this little lady and her gutter talk." I gave Porsche the evil eye. "Quiet down, missy, or I'll toss you in your cage and hang a sheet on it."

She peered at me disdainfully with one pale yellow eye, then turned her proud head to stare at me haughtily with the other. We had issues. When Cochraine took his wife down with him on a five to ten, I promised her we'd take good care of Porsche. If the female African Grey had simply fallen for Popeye, as expected, the temporary foster home would have been much happier. As it was, my baby had stopped charming everyone with his clever commentary and witty remarks, and the foster kid had started freaking out the neighborhood. Some of my neighbors probably thought I'd hooked myself up with a foul-mouthed pimp from the 'hood.

Which is kind of funny if you don't take it too seriously. And if you don't care that you never get invited to block parties.

"Why can't men and women get along?" my assistant wondered aloud.

I laughed while I wiped the bird shit from my foot with a clean section of newspaper. "You and I are about to 'get along' just fine, thank you."

And then you'll leave. Wham, bam, thank you ma'am. The only way to get along with one another, it seemed. You get your physical needs met together, your emotional needs met elsewhere.

A few minutes later, I followed him into the house. I snapped on a couple floor lamps in the living room and dropped my bag on the couch. I heard the shower running so I took the hint and went with it.

The bedroom was dark, and I left it that way. As I hurried through the high-ceilinged and airy room to the master bath, I quickly stripped off my clothes, discarding items as I went. My heart sped up as I pictured hunky Ringo in my shower, soaped up and ready for me. The door to the bathroom was open, and I walked right in.

The night was beginning to steam up, all right.

Lucky for me, I have a good-sized shower stall with three separate heads that give out powerful blasts of hundred and fifteen degree water. The foggy glass doors masked any activity behind it, but I was guessing Ringo was done scrubbing and was just waiting for me to join him. We both liked our sex wet and slippery. And steamy hot.

Just thinking about him, my hungry man assistant, so close, so ready for me, made me catch my breath. I was sort of panting, and my nipples hardened. I stopped long enough to towel off the bottom of the oval mirror over the porcelain sink. I needed to check my face. No sudden attack of zits, no stray food in my teeth, no drunken smile on my face. Well, sort of a drunken smile on my face. I pouted my lips in a sultry manner, brushed my wild hair out of my eyes, and headed for the shower.

Ringo slid open the door. "Aha. Just the woman I been expecting."

His black eyes danced. His muscles popped and shone under the fluorescent lighting. His erection was working its way up to full mast.

Did I mention how big Ringo is? He's huge. All over.

I grinned and slid in beside him. He was slippery, hot, and hard. All over.

Turning my back to show him my second best side, I demanded, "Soap me up, big boy."

My assistant complied readily with a gooey bar of shea butter soap. I love shea butter. It leaves your skin smooth as ice cream. I closed my eyes while his large hands traveled across my skin, pressing gently on my shoulders, back, buttocks, and thighs, smoothly easing over to caress my breasts, belly, and all my trigger points until I had to lean against him for support. My knees were shaking in anticipation.

Hot water cascaded off our bodies. I reached behind me for his fully erect member and cupped it, throbbing, against the crack in my ass. We stood like that for a moment, breathing heavily, wet, on the edge. Groaning, he pushed me forward with one gentle movement.

"Rinse off, unless you want me to have to lick the soapsuds off you." His voice was throaty, which turned me on even more.

"I'll take the spray off first, then the licking." I stepped directly under one of the pulsating shower heads.

Behind me, Ringo sank to his knees and reached for my hips. He maneuvered me into position, manipulating my legs, opening me up. I leaned forward and groaned when his fingers entered me and stroked my soaked lips, spreading them wider. My assistant knew his anatomy, or should I say he knew mine. He deftly positioned my dripping clit where we both wanted it.

The steamy water felt so good on my tight muscles, I hated to step out of the spray. But I knew what I needed to do. I bent over, forearms pressed against the shower tiles, my head on my arms. I was moaning like an overheated cat in a back alley. Still, Ringo touched me lightly. So damn lightly, patiently, teasing me, coaxing me to build up before release.

When his tongue entered me, I screamed in delight. I wasn't going to take more than a minute to come tonight. Ringo fluttered around and circled the hot spot, sucking me the way he knew drove me insane with desire. Just as I crested a wave of pure rush, he stopped.

I turned around, looked down. "What the fuck, Ringo?"

He was shivering. "I got knee pain like you wouldn't believe. Let's get out of the shower and hop into bed so I can finish what I was doin'."

"You better," I warned. "Or I'll have to fire your ass."

He stood up and grabbed me in a huge hug, kissing me passionately with those thick pink lips of his. His body smelled like melted butter, and his muscles were warm stones. His tongue tasted of coffee beans, draft beer, and me. I kissed him back. God, I loved kissing this man.

Eventually, we stepped out of the shower and dried each other with my only bath towel, a big fluffy thing from some big fluffy hotel I'd stayed in with my former husband. Arms around one another's cooling bodies, we stumbled into the master and tumbled onto my unmade bed. I should have been embarrassed to be such a domestic disaster, but I wasn't. Not at all. My assistant knew me. He knew what made me tick and what I considered unimportant. And he didn't care, as long as I took him inside me and we rocked for a good hard time.

So I did and we did. In fact, the second we hit the mattress, we got right down to business. And boy oh boy, business was good.

****

Two hours later, I sat out on the porch with a cup of chamomile tea. I was feeling pretty damn good. Ringo's the best assistant I've ever had. In every possible way. He totally gets me. He takes direction without protest. He works hard and plays nicely. He never asks to sleep over. He'll never start up post-coital discussions about where the relationship is headed. He fucks me passionately, romantically, the way I like it. Usually, I give the after-sex massage since his muscles get tense from sitting in parked cars all day, but whenever I need one he does the honors. After that, he goes home.

The birds dozed on their separate perches, eyes fluttering between half-open and closed. I loved looking at their tender eyelids, the tissue pale as an infant's fingernail. Every once in a while, one or the other would rustle delicate feathers. I wondered if they were dreaming about flying. Their wings aren't clipped, but they don't get an opportunity to spread them. Sad, what we do to nature. Tame it, cage it, shut it down, until all that's left is the dream of our innate potential.

Palm trees rustled in the breeze. The night air was soft and briny. My place is less than a mile from the beach, and when the wind blows in from the east, it smells like salted clams. You can't beat Florida on a winter night.

Eventually, I lay down on the rattan sofa, a moldy relic left over from my married days, but I wasn't going to fall asleep. Insomnia sucks when you have it, but it's great for doing stake-outs. It's also good for thinking things through. I can accomplish my best case analysis when I can't sleep, which is to say on most nights. Sometimes I wonder if I were able to sleep normally whether my life would be more normal as well. Maybe I'd be doing something else with my time. Maybe I would've pursued higher education, become a therapist, an avian vet, an investigative journalist. Instead of a worst case PI and a hired gun for burn victim women.

I believe in my work, and it's fulfilling in its way. It provides me with a deep sense of purpose. I feel I'm providing a service to those in dire need. But sometimes I wish I had a more ordinary job description. I've forgotten how it feels to enjoy an everyday life, one in which the homicides take place only in the newspaper and on the six o'clock news.

Like everyone who's been doing the same job year after year, I fantasize about doing something else with my time. After thousands of hours spent listening to the breathless sobs of the heartbroken, I've come to the conclusion that we're up against some very rough odds. Like Dr. Trainor says, it's biology, stupid. Men cheat because their brains make them do it. They're hardwired to seek variety in partners because they've been designed to spread their sperm around. It's in their genetic code. The male inhales the heady scent of a young, hormone-rich female, and they're compelled by their DNA to respond. Even when they're paired up or, as we women like to think, already taken. *This one's mine* does not apply to the primal drive to reproduce wildly. So, all our rules and bonds, our legal documents and religious vows, all the visits to Victoria's Secret cannot keep the male animal in the cage. They will run off and fly free, they will fuck around on us, and we can do little to stop them.

I want to believe in romance and happily ever after, but between the science and my work, it's damn near impossible. If you listen to Dr. Trainor, he'll tell you how only ten percent of primates practice monogamy, and a mere three percent of mammals remain mated for the long haul. According to the latest research, even those rare species we think of as monogamous for life actually aren't. Given the opportunity, almost all animals will fool around, looking for better genetic options for future offspring. Improving the line. When it comes to long-lasting mating behavior, the numbers are shockingly low.

So why am I running a business with such meager odds of providing a happy ending for my clients? I don't think of myself as a glass half-full sort of person, but I do want to believe in something. I want to believe that love can work out for the best. At least once in a while. And when it doesn't, I want to be able to provide for the victims of broken promises. I do what I can for the individual whose heart got crushed.

I don't share Dr. Trainor's nihilist Darwinism with my clients. They're in too much pain to understand the implications of the hard science of evolutionary biology. They're taking their losses personally. Instead, I try to comfort women in their grief and confusion while offering words of encouragement and hope. Everyone deserves to have hope, right? What I never say to my clients is this—we cannot tame the male drive to dominate, roam, reproduce. We can't even control ourselves. All we can do is make our men pay up. Serial monogamy is as good as it gets. If you've had him to yourself for more than a few years, count yourself among the lucky ones.

When my phone rang, I wasn't asleep. I was thinking about the three different kinds of love—sexual passion, romance, and pair bonding. I was wondering who ever said it was possible to find all three within a single relationship. Whoever started that rumor deserved a silver-toed boot in the butt. Because even a hard-ass realist like myself is incapable of letting that fantasy go.

I wasn't always such a hard-ass. Growing up with a working mom in a beat-down part of town, I might have kept my edges rough. Instead, I sharpened myself to a fine point, doing everything right. Evolving into the type of girl who separated the whites from the darks whenever she did the laundry, washing all the delicates by hand. As instructed.

But that was then. Now, I toss everything in the washtub together, see how it all comes out. Still, some of those early dreams linger.

I had one eye half-open, the other closed. I had to struggle to a sitting position, then feel around for my cell in the pocket of my terry cloth robe. Three-thirty in the morning. Had to be Ashton from one of the county's many familiar police stations. Or a client in serious emotional turmoil.

Fortunately for my soon to be ex, for whom my patience was stretched anorexically thin, the caller was all business.

"Ms. Treme?" she said in a whisper.

I sighed. "Yes?"

"Can we kill him tonight?"

"No, Mrs. Emworth," I responded, equally softly but firmly. I pictured a handsome gray-haired husband beside her on their eighty-count Egyptian cotton sheets. His steady breathing filled the well-appointed room. He slept the warm, deep sleep of the conscienceless while she lay there hour after hour, stiff and icy in the darkness, every untouched inch of her Pilates-toned body aching with grief. "I'm sorry, Mrs. Emworth, but you'll need to complete the cooling off period."

"He reeks of her," my client said. "I feel like putting a pillow over his head and sitting on it." She was breathing heavily, like she'd been on a treadmill. "I'm afraid I'll never make it through the entire month. Can I tell you what happened tonight? I'm sorry, but you did say twenty-four/seven."

"I wasn't asleep, no worries," I reassured her. "Are you able to talk freely right now?"

"Yes, I'm alone. I'm down in the kitchen. He's upstairs, asleep. With a big smile on his face, the bastard." She spoke quickly in a low voice, and I had to strain to hear. "I did what you said, but it didn't work. It was the most humiliating experience of my life."

I cringed. I'd had a few too many nights like that. Most women have. Perhaps because she was so gorgeous, my client had managed to avoid the degradation of failed seduction. Until now.

"Go on," I said.

She sucked in her breath before continuing. I wondered whether she was smoking a cigarette, possibly a joint. I couldn't blame her, but neither fit the image I had of her. In my mind, Mrs. Emworth belonged in a Bogart film from the 1940s, playing the role of the tragically beautiful woman in need of rescue. The victim who's been ensconced in an impenetrable ice cube, surrounded by the glittery sheen of enormous wealth.

"I went to lunch," she told me, "and I asked my close girlfriends to advise me on this next step. They've all been through the other woman ordeal at least once. They told me what to buy, what to do when he got home from work. They were helpful and encouraging.

Like you were." She sniffed. "Then I had my man drive me to the mall. I ended up with quite a few outfits, the kind of sexy getups you see in those cheesy porn films." She snorted. "God, I can't believe the things they sell now at the upscale shops. Used to be you had to buy this kind of stuff through the mail and the package would arrive discretely wrapped in brown paper."

She sighed. Maybe this wasn't her first attempt at playing to a mate's wildest fantasies.

"Blood red, neon pink, black lace. Tons of lace. Crotchless panties, thongs, G-strings in rainbow colors. Pasties, a cone bra that fits like a glove and makes my breasts look futuristic. Oh, my god. Then I found another store at the mall with all sorts of, well, *devices*. Battery-operated gizmos. A small whip. Plastic handcuffs. I went all out."

I pictured my client dressed like a dominatrix. The honey hair, the perfect skin, the double-D breasts. What man could resist?

A husband, of course. Her own husband.

"Before I got dressed, undressed, whatever you want to call it, I had Angela whip up a blender full of piña coladas. Finn always drinks them when we vacation in the islands. I was creating atmosphere, like you said. I made sure to tell Angela and Jojo to take the night off. I acted so happy and silly, I think they thought I'd gone nuts. Maybe I have."

"We all do in these situations," I said. "Insanity is normal right now—"

This didn't seem to reassure her. She spoke over me, continuing with her story. "So I really primped myself up. Styled my hair in the schoolgirl braids he's always liked, gave myself the Princess Grace does Heidi look. I put on extra makeup, lots of blush everywhere, a new scent. I even shaved everything off, and I mean *everything*."

Here she paused to gauge my reaction. "Good idea," I said.

Men who've been sleeping with young women tend to get used to the prepubescent look. I guess they like feeling they're with a virgin or something. Who knows what the hell they're thinking, *if* they're thinking.

"I dressed in candy-cane striped underthings and a pair of white go-go boots. The entire outfit was ludicrous. When I looked at myself in the full-length mirror in my dressing room, I was horrified." I could hear the embarrassment in her voice. "But I didn't back down. No, I lit a bunch of candles, put on a CD. Kenny G, for god's sake. Finn actually likes the guy." She clucked in disgust. At his musical taste or at her own behavior, I wasn't sure. "I sat on the edge of our bed and drank coladas until ten o'clock. He never called to say he'd be late. Not even to lie and say he was still working. He didn't even bother to lie."

Okay, now I knew where we stood. The marriage was crumbling. It sounded like it was in the final stages. Perhaps Mrs. Emworth was right, we might be forced to speed up the schedule. If a husband moves out before we're ready to move in, we have to abandon the plan. A death soon after a breakup can shed a shadow of suspicion on the widow. Ex-Treme Measures will not allow any suspicion to be cast upon our clients. None. Shadows on them means the high beam on us, and we can't have that.

My client sucked in some air, steadied her voice. She was attempting to be brave, keeping her cool while recounting disaster. "I heard him come in. He stomped around down in the foyer and called out for me. He sounded drunk. And ebullient, the way he is after a good fucking. When I said I was upstairs, he tromped up. I could hear the spring in his step, like he'd left twenty-five years in that girl's snatch."

I laughed, but I covered the phone so she wouldn't hear me. That was a good one. I'd have to remember to share it with Ringo.

"You should've seen his face when he walked into our bedroom and saw me sitting there, looking like Linda Lovelace. Like a pole dancer from the Pussycat Lounge. He raised those cocky eyebrows of his and he said, 'What's this? Were we invited to a costume party? Sorry to miss it, darling, but you look absolutely ridiculous.' Then he stumbled into the bathroom and locked the door behind him. Locked it, like I was going to rush in and rape him while he was in the shower. Scrubbing off the cheap scent of that little girl's discount cologne."

She waited for my reaction, so I gave her one. "He sounds like a lost cause. If you can stomach it, keep up the charade. If you can't do it, well, you don't *have* to keep at it. Although I do think you might find him more responsive if you were to lure him out of town."

I waited while she grunted a noncommittal response.

I tried to talk to her, but my words were meaningless compared to whatever was going on inside her head and heart. My advice, sound as it might be, was unlikely to help her pain. Only time could heal that wound. Time and revenge.

"Look, it's very difficult for a wife to compete against someone younger, fresher, and more willing to ignore all the issues a man might have. If he'd already spent the evening in a twenty-year-old's bed, he probably knew he'd be unable to perform with you. To cover up, he insulted you and fled. Please believe me, Mrs. Emworth. It's not you. It's basic biology."

She sighed deeply. After a moment, she said, "I don't care what it costs. I want that man dead."

Chapter Five

My first Ex-Treme client was a Palm Beach beauty whose family was worth millions. Millicent Madreau had come to me at the recommendation of her sister, who had recently lost a real louse of a husband in a private plane crash. I couldn't take responsibility for the accident, but I had been investigating the man's antics. I guess I wasn't the only one in the county who wanted the conman dead. Millie's sister had adapted readily to her widowhood, finding the kind of release you read about in books about spiritual rebirth.

Tiny but not frail, Millie was a perfect little white doll. Her delicate looks were accompanied by a Southern grace and charm you no longer find in women. Especially here in nasty South Florida. The children were the kind of beautiful blonds you see in magazine ads for expensive kids' clothes.

Millie's husband was a horror story. Six four, fifty pounds overweight, bald, and red faced. He breathed like a rhino, talked two decibels too loud, and forced himself on a room. He made her life miserable. He made everybody's life miserable.

Does this sound like a cliché? It is, but there's a reason for that. Such stereotypes do exist. In every economic strata. And the woman in this particular brand of sad couple is usually fucked.

She asked me to find out who he was sleeping with

so I took her money and I followed him for a month. This was pre-Ringo so I was on my own. I didn't know then that I needed an assistant. I didn't even know I would kill him. And so many others to follow.

A financial advisor, he'd made his money the old fashioned way. He stole it from his elderly clients. Who knows why they listened to him. Looking at him, you'd know right away he was full of himself, bloated on his own hot air. But he had presence and a kind of simmering power. The feeble elderly lined up to give him their savings.

The first week told me nothing I could use. He worked all day, he went home every night at six. He sat in the back of a sleek black Lincoln and talked on the phone until the car stopped at the sprawling manse end of a looping drive. He was still on the phone when he got out of the car and hefted his bulk up the front stairs.

A cookie cutter mansion on the Intracoastal. Interchangeable with all the other mega mansions in Palm Beach. Pink and white like a shell. Hollow as a conch. Fragile enough that a big wave could toss it out to sea.

I watched from my perch behind the ficus hedge in the back yard. All those French doors, and I never saw him hug one of the adorable kids or speak to his beautiful wife. He went from his office in a stone building in Gulf Stream to his chrome and leather home office, then back again. The man holed up like a rodent.

My client claimed her husband had a lover, and she planned to ditch him on those grounds. But I couldn't see it. The man was a boor and a workaholic, but on the cheating charts he sure looked clean.

The second week on his trail was exactly like the

first only he worked until eight every night. All the way home, cell phone to the ear. With a bug implanted in the car, now I could listen in. It was all business all the time. Buy, sell, sell, buy. Reassuring clients that profits were still up. Checking in with legal advisors. Bullshitting endlessly. Yawn.

But on the philandering front, he was clean as the white ibis dotting his wide green lawn.

Next up, I set a trap. To see if his eyes wandered when confronted with opportunity. Most men's eyes do wander. So do their hands. And their dicks. This is not proof of prior cheating behavior. Just biology at work. But I needed to get a sense of the man. As a man.

The outfit was ridiculous. Short black skirt, tall black shoes, see-through black silk blouse. White bra. White garters just above the abbreviated hemline. I mean, really? He would've had to be blind not to stare.

I parked the rental car in the middle of the road just half a block from his house. When his driver rounded the bend, he had to stomp hard on the brakes. I leaned into the front end, my head under the open hood, my ass on flagrant display. In slow motion, I turned and waved. Mouthed the word *help*.

He did not get out of the car. His driver fiddled around under my hood, replacing what I'd detached. In a gruff voice he told me to try to start the car. It roared to life. Another piece of shit American-made car, all ready to rock and ride.

The driver had his own charms. Dark, wiry, smelling of lemon and cigarettes. He leaned in the driver's side window and whispered, "I'd give my eye teeth to fuck you tonight."

I smiled and told him my husband was on the West

Palm force, but he was welcome to come over and give it a shake. With a sorry look in his inky eyes, he nodded his head. Then he hurried back to the limo and got in.

Millie's husband was still on the phone. His eyes had skated over me like I was black ice. Like I didn't exist unless I made him fall down.

I was ready to advise my client to look for another reason to divorce her husband, as I was sure there were many, but the next day he surprised me. It was a Thursday, bright and clear with a cool ocean breeze. When the sun came up, I was already waiting at the end of his street with a cup of tepid coffee.

He left at the usual time, but not in the usual manner. He drove himself past me in a convertible Austin-Healy, red with a jaunty black stripe. He drove fast. He was not on the phone.

I followed him up the coast to Jupiter. Then over the bridge to the island. I stayed back. I didn't want him to ID me. My car was different, so was my outfit. Still, I couldn't take any chances. There was something about the man. I wanted to find out what it was before he found out who I was.

He parked in the loop of a driveway for a ridiculous monstrosity of a house overlooking the ocean. Had to be ten thousand square feet of marble with pillars to nowhere and multiple decks. And an awful lot of blue glass.

I parked my VW two blocks away in a thick stand of slash pine, pulling my car in deep, tucking it off the street. Hoping I would not get towed.

I entered the property on foot, slinking around in the sea grape bushes that surrounded the pool area. I heard voices. A man's deep growl. And a young woman's giggle. A very young woman's giggle. Several very young women's soft little giggles.

When I peeked through the foliage, I was glad I was unarmed. Because I would have shot him right there, right then.

Millicent's husband was being tended to by a group of girls. Twelve, thirteen year old girls. Poorly fed and underdeveloped children from an Asian country, probably Vietnam or Thailand. They were all pale little things with barely budding breasts and no pubic hair. Naked little girls with their soft hands and soft mouths on the bloated body of a fifty year old swine.

I gagged. I took my photos. I left, cursing under my breath.

Now I was worried about Millie's children. Men like that, they stop at nothing. They don't believe they have to. The rules do not apply.

When I showed the photos to Millie, she crumpled like an origami bird. I held her delicate body in my arms while she wept.

Finally, she wiped her tears and looked at me. Her eyes were as clear and blue as the water in the Jupiter Inlet. "I want that fucker killed."

I nodded. I knew how she felt. With all his money, he'd be able to keep the law at bay. He would never go to jail for his actions. He'd always be on the loose, a menace to her and her kids. A menace to women and children everywhere.

"I'll see what I can do," I told her.

Less than a week later, Millie's husband died of a heart attack. The kind that can be brought on by a curare dart to the back of the neck while one is driving a convertible sports car on the way to a party with sex slave children. The kind of heart attack all men like that deserve.

****

After lying in bed staring up at the lopsided rattan ceiling fan, which was whirring in an unbalanced hum like a madman in a backyard workshop, I realized I could neither sleep nor analyze. So I got up and changed into running shorts and a bra top, then set out for a run in the darkness.

I zipped through the silent town, heading down faintly lit streets to A1A, then across the empty highway to the beach. Clumps of black and white gulls stood together, all facing in the same direction. Since the sun was not yet up, the air was blissfully cool. It was quiet, serene, starry.

I ran north, kicking sand and breathing salt until the sweat stung my eyes. Plovers and sandpipers scurried across the wet sand, stopping to poke around in their spastic search for breakfast items. I jogged past them, then ran home for my own morning meal.

Cereal and almond milk, coffee as strong as I could take it. I read yesterday's paper and goofed off for a bit.

By the time I'd showered off and fed my parrots their brown rice cakes, chopped figs, and diced mango, I was late. I jumped into my car and chugged to the office as fast as the eggbeater motor would take me. My Cabriolet convertible is from 1992, so it doesn't move too fast. I could have run to work at a better clip.

Ringo was standing out front waiting for me. I parked across the street. Ex-Treme Measures operates out of a low-rise brick office building a few blocks northwest of downtown. The neighborhood is down at the heels and, to be politically incorrect, I'd have to say the area is *hoody*. However, the location works for us. The streets are quiet, the people distant yet nonthreatening. Nobody butts into your business, but everybody knows it. Community isn't the right word. Camaraderie might be closer to the truth.

Across from the office, seagulls swooped and dropped like little white bombs into an empty lot. While I was locking the car door, I waved to the guys who hung out there. A few of them waved back. "Watch your junker for a nickel," somebody joked.

I laughed. "I think I'll save my money, hold out for an insurance claim."

A thin guy with super long dreadlocks said, "Good luck with that shit," and we all chuckled.

Ringo handed me my take-out double latté and opened the front door, allowing me to pass in front of him.

"You're awfully gentlemanly today," I said. "What's with that?"

He grinned. "You deserve the royal treatment. After all, aren't you the best lay in town?"

"Objection. Leading the witness," I said, apropos of nothing.

"Overruled. Hey, this isn't a trial. At least, it doesn't feel that way to me."

I reassured him by patting his upper arm, then grabbed on tight for a few seconds. I was, I'll admit, copping a feel. I imagined him at LA Fitness, pumping two-eighty and thinking about our nights together.

My horniness barometer began to rise, swift and sharp, so I removed my hand. "Got a call from the new client last night. You were smart to hang on to that fifty."

The lobby floor squeaked under our shoes. It was dingy but heavily waxed. We crossed the deserted room and headed for the stairs. Ringo and I were usually the first to arrive in the building, and we liked it that way. There were other small businesses operating around us—a web designer, a small home insurance company, a holistic pediatrician. But we'd had little interaction with the owners or employees. Curt nods, brief hellos, that was about it. For reasons of privacy, we liked it this way.

On the stairs, Ringo said, "So she can't make it through the cooling off period?"

"Doesn't look like it. I'm wondering—"

"Nope, don't even go there. I disagree, as always. Give it the full cool down before we hit him. I really hate it the way you girls give up so fast. What's wrong with talkin' it out, tryin' to understand *his* side of the story? Some of these poor guys don't know what hit 'em or why."

When I turned around to argue, I caught my assistant checking out my assets. He seemed riveted. True, my skinny jeans were ridiculously tight, and running for two decades has done wonders for my glutes, but I stopped on the landing and waited for him to step up beside me. We had work to do, and we both needed to stay focused.

"Of course, they don't know who or why. That's the point, to surprise them. Another few weeks is unlikely to change this woman's mind. She's over it."

My assistant understood I was the expert at judging readiness in our clients. He couldn't help himself, though. He always empathized with the husbands. Bros befo' hos, as Porsche would say. If I listened to Ringo, we'd never ex-terminate any of the bad husbands. We'd be just another investigation agency with stacks of ugly photos worth a few thousand here, a few thousand there. We'd be offering Band-Aids instead of euthanasia. A temporary patch instead of the option to buy a whole new outfit.

"If we wait too long, you know we can't go in," I cautioned. "Not if there's any chance the situation will turn on our client."

"Well, we got the other issue to consider this time. If Mrs. Cantor gets pegged for what just happened to her husband, they'll eventually take a look at us. A close look. We're the private investigation firm she hired to snoop on him, the one that informed her he was involved in a steamy bromance."

He had a point, of course. We were juggling two hot potatoes, and my hands were burning.

I hurried ahead, and Ringo followed at my heels. He was right on top of me all the way down the hall. I turned around once and said, "You're like a puppy today, snuffing my butt. It's making me nervous."

He shrugged. "Can't be helped. Since you're in the lead, since you insist on being alpha dog, your very fine ass is what's keepin' me on track." He waited for me to unlock the office door before he added, "Any chance for another late-day meeting at the Tam?"

"Not a chance." I flicked on the lights and the ceiling fan. "Not two nights in a row. Against house rules."

"Objection." Ringo set his cardboard cup on the coffee table and wrapped his arms around me. "I object on the grounds that it's cruel and unusual punishment.

Inhumane treatment. Of a poor, innocent sled dog."

Horn dog was more like it. He smelled of suntan oil and minty toothpaste, with a dash of Colombian coffee beans. I inhaled deeply before I stepped away. "Don't tempt me. They do make cages big enough for brutes your size, you know."

"Kinky."

I pulled the lid off my cup and changed the subject back to the business at hand. "So I need you to follow up on Mrs. Emworth today. Also, we've got to deal with Mr. Cantor. Can you check in with your friend at the morgue? She needs to be on the lookout. Cantor could come in at any time and in any kind of condition."

"Right, I'm on it. I already ran that phone number and got an address for the guy Mrs. Cantor used. I'll run by there later today."

"I'll take it," I said. The coffee was waking me up. "I can swing by right now. My first appointment isn't until noon. Where's our Mr. Grey live?"

"Boca Raton, Deerfield line. Condo on A1A." He grinned. "Nice day for a *long* drive."

My assistant meant it would take me longer to get there than if he took the assignment. He loved to tease me about how my car couldn't go over forty, but I took his jibes in good humor. I was fond of the rolling piece of crap. If it wasn't so girlie, I would have named my car. We were that tight.

"Oh, and Grey's real name is Dickensen. Brad Dickensen." He handed me a printout with the background info on Mrs. Cantor's hitman.

The guy had your typical pro go-to background. Ex-Marine, ex-cop, ex-security guard, our competitor worked for Robes, Pierre. One of the largest law firms in the state, the company's cloned herd of button-down attorneys represented corporate bigwigs caught with their hands in the till, bad boy playboys involved in drunken hit and runs, and "retired" Mafia kingpins. Mrs. Cantor's Mr. Grey, who was legally known as Brad Dickensen, was employed as a contractor for the law firm. He'd worked for them for the last eight months. From prior experience with shady law firms, we knew that his job description there could include anything from bodyguard for rich scumbags to internal spy to, well, hitman.

I was surprised. She'd hired a professional. So why had he behaved so unprofessionally?

Ringo dumped his empty coffee cup in the wastebasket by my desk and headed for the door. "See if you can work up your Irish thirst while you're baking your freckles out on A1A."

He wasn't one for giving in easily. Making him an excellent investigator and a pain in the ass lover. As he waved from the doorway, my fuck buddy added a parting shot. "You know you want me. Might as well give in to it."

He closed the door just in time. The legal pad I tossed at his head bounced off the hollow wood and onto the carpet. I could hear him laughing. I'm pretty sure he strutted down the hall to the stairs.

Men. Can't live without them, can't kill them. Oh, wait, you *can* kill them.

I retrieved the legal pad and tore off all the pages I'd crumpled in my burst of temper. It was all so predictable, the biology of attachment. Every time we make love, our bodies release chemicals.

Neurochemicals like oxytocin, vasopressin, prolactin, dopamine. All we have to do is touch one another, and our neurology creates a bond between us. We satisfy our affect hunger drive this way, with loving one another. But it never lasts. So why couldn't we just have sex and skip attachment entirely? Why did it always have to end in love, romance, disaster?

I shook my head. I needed Ringo. He was important to my business. He was also a worthwhile addition to my bed now and again. I really didn't want either of us to ruin a good thing by pretending there was something else going on. The truth was, there was nothing more than innate biology between us. And that was enough. Wasn't it?

I sat down at my computer and did a search on Brad Dickensen. Lexus-Nexus, county tax rolls, local court documents. I found nothing more than Ringo had provided. No images, no family photos on Facebook or Pinterest, no shots of the ex-dick at Robes, Pierre company picnics or on the roster for the firm's softball team.

No surprise there. You won't find much on me online, either.

I had little to go on but his home, current and former work addresses. So what? I locked up and headed for the stairs. I was looking forward to the excursion. It was, as my assistant had said, a beautiful day for a long drive.

Chapter Six

There are spots along A1A that still take my breath away, even though I've driven the beach route thousands of times. Personally, I don't know any real live *native* Floridians. Those folks are rare as native plants in this part of the state. But I'd bet even the people who've been here all their lives find the clean white sand and tropical teal water just as awesome as I do.

When I first moved to South Florida to be with Ashton, I went to the beach every single day to stare at the horizon. Frothy or flat, navy or turquoise, agitated or calm, the ocean inspired me. I felt as if the changing tide shared its moods with me. I fell in love and vowed to myself I'd run the beach daily.

I haven't kept my vow. Most people don't. But I do run the beach often. And I still love the ocean. I'll always love South Florida. Not because of the people. They're mostly rude assholes. I don't know why, but studies show there are more dickwads per square mile in South Florida than anywhere else on the planet.

I'm sort of joking about that, but the truth is, the people here tend toward the truly awful. However, I've been willing to set that fact aside. Because I'll always have plenty of clients in a place like this. And I'll always have the beach.

From Linton Boulevard south, A1A was clogged

with traffic. Mostly snowbirds and tourists, crawling along, rubbernecking at the breathtaking ocean view. It was no use honking at them to go the speed limit. What would be the point? My car shook at forty. If I floored it, which I never did, I'd probably blow a rod.

Fortunately, the water was a mind-blowing shade of glittering aquamarine with a dusting of whitecaps. I watched the foam lather coming from the unending, rippling waves. The crash of the tide created a womblike mantra, and it soothed me.

The sky was cloudless, the humid air full of the smell of jasmine and brine. A heady combination. It reminded me of sex, so I turned on the radio to take my mind off my private life. I could not let this thing with Ringo turn into something we'd both regret. Like living together or, god forbid, falling in love. I needed him. I trusted him. He was important to me. It would be insane to fuck that up just because we were good in bed.

And oh, were we good in bed. Really good. Which meant it wouldn't last. Couldn't last. There was no way we could enjoy lust, romance, *and* a solid bond. He was a male. The clock was already ticking on his interest, our coupling. Soon enough, disaster would loom over us.

I forced myself to think about work. How could I approach the hitman, find out what he'd done with Mr. Cantor's body, if anything? He could be lying to Mrs. Cantor. That would have to be determined. Direct questioning seemed to be the only option. There exists an unspoken hitperson code of honor. If I couldn't get him to talk to me on that level, I might have to snoop around his place, see what I could find. Getting access to the condo building might be tricky, depending on the level of security. But I had my ways.

When I spotted the building on the east side of the road, I turned into the long, circular drive. Wow, some fancy shit. Everything was so green. Emerald tile fountains, manicured lawn, royal palms over fifty feet tall. And a mint-green security booth with tinted windows.

How could a law firm flunky afford this kind of luxury condo? I'd expected one of the crumbling oldies from the 1960s, those towering apartment buildings, each with a thousand units, all built for the Jews from Long Island. I'm not being prejudiced when I say this, just historically accurate about the population that moved down to South Florida during the mass migration of the postwar years. A lot of them still own property on the beach. Or their offspring do.

A young security guard opened the sliding glass door of his mini-office and approached my car. Tall, blond, bony. He had a side arm. They all do now. You could never tell when a ninety-year-old Holocaust survivor was gonna try to take down the building with a high-powered automatic or an old hand grenade or something.

"Hi there." I flashed my brightest, most girly smile. "Maybe you can help me. I'm looking for a Mr. Brad Dickensen in apartment six-oh-six?"

"Do you have an appointment?" The guard was barely out of high school. His voice shook, and there were zits scattered across his pale forehead. He needed to get out of that sunless booth and hit the health club, the local Whole Foods Market. "I don't have any names on the visitors' list for Mr. Dickensen today."

"I didn't realize I had to call ahead," I cooed. "I'm

actually trying to get an appointment to meet with him, and he's been ignoring my calls. Thought if I dropped by to meet him in person..."

I actually fluttered my eyelashes. Ridiculous, but the maneuver had worked for Cleopatra and Elizabeth Taylor. Who was I to deny history's many past successes?

He looked away, fiddling with his handgun. "I'm not supposed to tell anyone this, but you can park two blocks up in the public lot and walk the beach back. Like about twenty minutes ago, I saw Mr. Dickensen in the lobby. He had a bathing suit on, and he was oiled up. If you get what I'm sayin'."

"I do. I do," I gushed.

Should I tip the guy or would that make him rethink his security breach? I decided to thank him with my female charms instead, so I reached out and grabbed his upper arm. Wow, it was like holding a drumstick. He flinched, poor kid, then flushed an amazing shade of tomato red.

"You are a true gentleman," I flattered, rubbing his bicep, or what passed for one.

Where had the peachy Georgia accent come from? I patted his shirtsleeve for a few seconds more before I let go. His eyes bulged and, I swear, his tongue lolled.

"Thank you so much, honey," I said before I pulled away.

In the rearview, I watched him standing there for a second before shaking himself off like a wet dog. He walked slowly back to his glass prison. Poor kid didn't get out enough. If he did, he'd be mincemeat. The South Florida women would chew that guy up and spit him out like he had a hundred thousand carbohydrate calories.

The public parking lot was crowded. Nine o'clock and sunny…what did I expect? I eased my little car into a non-spot on the grass beyond the city residents' parking area, crossing my fingers the park rangers wouldn't ticket me. You need a resident pass for the public beach lots, and they crack down on cheaters in the busy winter season. If the cops ticketed me, there would be a public record of my activity in the vicinity. I didn't like it, but there was nothing I could do.

An essential part of this business is the ability to come prepared. I always plan ahead, and you can tell by looking at the things I carry with me. I unlocked the trunk of my car and rummaged around until I found the canvas beach bag holding my spare bikini, an oversize towel, flip flops, and a tube of top-level sunblock. Then I headed to the public restrooms to get in costume.

Out on the hot sand, the off-shore breeze felt good on my warm skin. But the bikini was from 2006, and it crept up my ass as I walked south toward "Mr. Grey's" condo building. I wrapped the blue striped towel around my waist like a skirt, then jogged a little, scattering flocks of tiny sandpipers skittering along the shoreline. It was easy to recognize the building—green tint glass windows overlooking thirty-foot patios. High end luxury sandwiched between patchy remnants of the postwar middleclass ghetto.

The pool was small, but it jutted out, greedy for more beachfront. Bright neon umbrellas advertising several brands of import beers shaded the deck. An overly tanned man sat by himself on a chaise lounge, his oiled skin shimmering, greasy as a slab of bacon. He looked familiar, but I couldn't place him, especially because I was squinting against the harsh glare from the white sand.

Casually removing my towel skirt in order to offer a complete view of my near-naked torso, I mounted the short wooden stairway that led to the condo pool deck. Mr. Dickensen did not look up from his paperback, not even after I let myself in, entering the pool area through the squeaky gate.

Some security. Junior in the glass booth out front wasn't the only way to breach this building.

An elderly couple sat under one of the umbrellas playing cards. Their skin hung off in freckled folds, and their spotted knees touched intimately. They smiled at one another across the plastic table, sharing long looks of tender amusement. Were they newly mated or lifelong partners? Why didn't they want to kill one another? I felt like interviewing them, grilling them about their secrets on tolerating their relationship.

When I blocked Dickensen's sun, he reluctantly tore his eyes from the book in his lap. A long minute later, he closed it with a sigh. *Fifty Shades*, the third book in the series.

I continued to stare down at him without speaking. My mind sped through a range of reactions before settling on hilarity. Fortunately, before I began laughing, I remembered where I'd seen Dickensen's face before. And his body.

"Mind if I sit?" I didn't wait for a response. I plopped down onto the plastic deck chair beside him. "How's the book? I hear it's gripping."

"I'm not in the mood to chitchat if you don't mind." His voice had a lilt to it, a mild accent of some kind. Minnesotan? Canadian?

As he reopened his bad novel, I said, "Neither am I, Mr. Dickensen. Or should I call you Mr. Grey?" I paused to let the knowledge I was dropping on him sink in. "I'm here on behalf of Bella Cantor. Steven Cantor's wife."

He looked at me blankly for a few seconds.

You know, Bella. The poor lady whose husband you seduced and killed. The one whose hard-earned paychecks from her low-wage garage job you fucking stole.

I kind of hate men sometimes. This was one of those times.

There's no one more full of shit than a cop, except maybe for an ex-cop. As Dickensen opened his mouth to lie, my cell buzzed. "This might be Mrs. Cantor," I lied.

If you can't beat 'em.

"Tell me," was how I answered the phone. Our code for speak softly, Vanna's got company.

"You with Dickensen?" Ringo asked.

"Are you talking about a homicide?" I said back, watching the melanoma candidate in the next chair for a response. He picked up his book and pretended to read. "Where'd they find the body?"

"We got problems, big problems," Ringo said. "How long you gonna be up in Boca?"

"See you in less than an hour," I promised before hanging up.

Dickensen continued to pretend to read his book. He didn't flip any pages. I couldn't see his eyes behind his Ray-Bans, but I was sure they weren't scanning the sexy words of the ultra-popular potboiler.

I was forced to put a halt to his silly pretense. Why

do some men make you lean in and slap them across the face? They ask for it, then act surprised.

"You're familiar with the Cantor family, right, Mr. Dick?" I said in a no-nonsense tone.

"That's Dick*ensen*," he responded, reluctantly closing the book. "Am I familiar with anyone named Cantor? Maybe yes. Maybe no. Maybe fuck off." We stared at one another until he heaved a weighted sigh. "Well, Miss Treme, I'm sure you wouldn't be here interrupting my private time on this private pool deck if you didn't have some fucking inadmissible evidence indicating I do know the delightful couple, Mr. and Mrs. Steven Cantor."

He forced a laugh, his spit-shined teeth a sharp contrast with his excessively bronzed skin. Some might see him as a handsome middle-aged man, with his thick crop of silver hair, high cheek bones, and personally trained physique. But the guy gave me the creeps. I hate excessively cool, conventionally good-looking men. They inflict more pain on females than any other kind of male. This is true in the animal kingdom, too. Female animals will go for older males with the glossy coats and bright feathers that indicate health, longevity, and good genes. This is often a good idea for breeding purposes, but a bad choice for long-term satisfaction. The better looking males are in demand, and they respond by enjoying multiple partners.

"If you're wondering how I know your name, Miss Treme, I'd be happy to explain our connection. It's quite complicated, however. You may want to settle back and listen."

I was perched on the edge of the uncomfortable chair, but not because I planned on jumping up to leave.

I just didn't want to spread my thighs all over the weave of the seat. Once I stood up, the latticework pattern on the backs of my legs would be so ugly it could be debilitating. I refused to walk the beach like that. I wasn't going to humiliate myself in public any more than I had to. A girl has her pride.

So I crossed my legs carefully, flexing my calves, and forced a smile. "I'm listening. But make it quick. I don't have all day. I work, Mr. Dick, to help my clients. Rather than fucking them and ripping off their wives."

To my surprise, he laughed. "Oh please. Let's not pretend we're on any moral high ground here, Miss Ex-Treme Measures. I may utilize different methods of operation than you do, but we're both in the same business. And we both do what we must in order to please our clients."

Shit. He'd done his homework, all right.

I gritted my teeth and said nothing. What could I say? He wouldn't believe me if I tried to compare our codes of conduct. He wouldn't buy it that I selected my clients with great care, only signing on to eliminate the most reprehensible of husbands. I didn't want to defend my innocence regarding sexual relationships with clients, either. After all, I *was* sleeping with my assistant. So there was no denying it, I was—in cop terms—a buddy fucker. Even though that wasn't the same thing as having an affair with a client. Even though I never slept while we were together. But I just didn't want to go there. So I didn't.

"Miss Treme—or may I call you Vanna?" He didn't wait for me to respond, he just kept talking. Because of the mirrored shades, I couldn't see if he was looking at me. But it felt like he was looking through me. "Vanna, you've got a rep in the field. I heard about you several years ago, when I worked out of a firm up north. They talked about your exclusivity, your clientele. A female, doing what we do, but on the other side of the fence. Making it work, making it pay."

He nodded, as if in approval, then frowned. My stock was heading down. "The people I work for now, however, they don't like it when a woman moves in on their action. Especially when she appears to be working for the other side. And in this case, with the Cantors, you appear to be working with the enemy."

Rivulets of perspiration dripped between my breasts. I wished we were in the shade like the old couple playing cards. Maybe we would be smiling at one another without the homicidal edge we both seemed to be displaying. Meanwhile, the sun was wreaking its scorchery on my Irish skin. And my scalp burned. It felt sweat-soaked and pinking. So much for washing my hair this morning, I shouldn't have bothered.

My patience, always in short supply, withered away. The *enemy*? I'd give this slippery bastard a goddam enemy.

Through teeth still gritted in a phony smile, I said, "I thought you worked for Robes, Pierre, the law firm. Why would *they* care what I'm up to? I'm self-employed and provide a service to my private clients. Why would anyone you know talk of my work, when what I do is help women in the throes of emotional crises?" My smile sizzled, blistering my lips. "There is no *action*, not unless you are speaking of lives ruined by cheating spouses. Right name, wrong job description. You must have me confused with someone else."

I was boiling on the inside, toasting on the outside. I could feel my skin crisping. I said, "My business is registered with the state of Florida as a private investigation firm. We specialize in domestic relations. That is, unfaithful spouses. Your friend Mr. Cantor is one of these. As you very well know." I paused, but only for dramatic effect. "You know this in the *biblical* sense, Dick—may I call you Dick?"

He might have reddened under the oily tan. I wasn't sure. His voice sharpened, though, and when he spoke it cut through me. "Mr. Cantor is seeking protection from a violent and unstable wife. Mrs. Cantor has threatened her husband's life more than once, and he is, understandably, afraid of her. His divorce papers have been drawn up by his lawyers. She needs to be restrained, possibly institutionalized. In the meantime, my clients have asked me to protect Mr. Cantor from his wife's insane desire to hurt him. This is exactly what I am doing."

He smoothed his slick, hairless chest with one manicured hand. A ringless hand. My ass was stuck to the hot plastic, and I knew I would make a disgusting slurp when I stood up, peeling myself from the seat. I stayed put.

Dick removed his shades and showed me his Paul Newman eyes. Nice, clear, and riveting, but I saw no mercy there. "We have evidence that Mrs. Cantor has tried to hire a professional hitman to kill my client, and that she has ordered the hit. This evidence is admissible in court."

My heart lurched around for a while, trying to find purchase in my chest. I returned Dick's cold stare, willing my eyes to form icicles in the still air between us. "Are you accusing me of conspiracy?"

He laughed. "Don't get your hot little bikini in a twist, Vanna. I'm not out to fuck with you. Or maybe I am, but not like that."

Gay guys shouldn't make insinuating comments to straight women. Especially good-looking gay guys. That kind of shit is just so misleading. Another reason for us to hate men.

His smile disappeared, and his eyes remained cold. "Mrs. Cantor is a significant threat, and we've got the evidence to prove it. You should do what's right for your business and notify her that you are no longer on the case. Before she gets herself arrested on a fifty-one/fifty, and sent to the mental ward where she belongs."

As the silvered shades slid back into place, he tilted his head, waiting for me to agree to comply with his thinly veiled threat. Either Ex-Treme Measures backed off, he was implying, or we'd be linked to Mrs. Cantor's illegal behavior and criminal intent. Even an accusation of conspiracy would not look good on our resume.

I said nothing. I had nothing to say. He had us where he wanted us. To underline his control over the situation, he picked up his book and opened it again. *Ouch.*

My phone buzzed, and I played with it until it stopped. Then I stood up, grimacing at the unpleasant sound of my damp thighs unsticking from the seat. I waited for him to look up, but he didn't.

"Bella hired *you* to kill her husband. And she has evidence that you and her husband are involved.

Sexually. How does this make Ex-Treme Measures culpable?"

I knew what he was going to say, but I wanted to hear him say it.

"You want to get involved in a criminal investigation, be my guest. If not, be a smart girl and fuck off. My firm knows how to handle the situation so that nobody gets hurt. Including you and your feminazi PI firm." He didn't even bother to look up from his reading material when he added, "And I do not appreciate being videotaped without my permission."

I turned off the camera on my phone and slunk off. If I'd had a tail, you know where it would have been.

Chapter Seven

The second Ex-Treme client followed the first by only a few months. I had just enough time to realize I didn't feel any remorse about popping off Millie's ex before another opportunity to help a woman in distress presented itself.

Sabrina Torrash strolled into my office on a Friday afternoon at quarter to five. She was that kind of woman. Thick black hair in dreads down to her beautiful butt. White teeth in a ready smile. Beautiful hands and feet in the prettiest pair of red hot Miu Miu heels I'd ever seen on a real person. Those shoes were fashion model glam.

"Where'd you get those amazing heels?" I asked her after we'd introduced ourselves and settled on the couch.

"I have a little shop on Clematis," she told me. "And I just opened another on the beach. I've done really well with previously owned clothing." She grinned and I had to smile in return. "The rich bitches in Palm Beach wouldn't dream of giving their used clothing to charity. They want good money for their castoffs. And everyone else is willing to pay it."

I nodded. I'd done my fair share of shopping for leftovers. I preferred used quality when I had a formal event that couldn't be avoided. After, I could always resell the outfit on consignment. Get back half of what

I'd paid. Still, it beat going to the mall.

"I've heard you're discreet," Sabrina said. "And that's what I need right now. Utmost discretion."

"Of course," I acknowledged, and with a tilt of my chin I encouraged her to continue.

"My husband is leaving me. He says there's nobody else, but I am fairly certain he's carrying on with my business partner. And if he is, I want him out of my life. But not her."

I must have looked surprised. Usually, a friend who cheats with one's spouse is fair game. Was she harboring no anger toward this other woman?

When I started to speak, Sabrina interrupted. "She's the money behind our business. She's not a friend, just a business associate. She's important to me. He's dispensable." Her smile contrasted with the spark of rage in her wide brown eyes. "If there's a way to out him without upsetting my business partner, I would like to pursue that avenue."

I nodded, but I wasn't at all sure how that could be arranged.

We agreed on a month of surveillance, and she cut me a check. "I'll set aside a really amazing pair of shoes for you. You wear a nine double A, right?"

I nodded enthusiastically. Sabrina didn't miss a trick.

Her suspicions were confirmed on the first afternoon of my surveillance when I followed Mr. Torrash from his store in downtown Delray to a luxury hotel on the beach in Deerfield. He was not meeting with a client interested in the high end stereo equipment he sold, that was obvious.

I hung out at the black marble bar and watched as

he sat by the window and worked on a single malt Scotch. His skin was so rich I was sure it must feel like velvet. He had dark broody eyes and a well-tended physique. I could see why she'd fallen for him. He had that sexy puppy dog look.

Eventually, the woman walked in. Sabrina's business partner. I recognized her from the photos I'd seen on the Internet.

I couldn't believe he'd drop his lovely wife for this nightmare. Short, plump, huge fake tits. A mean plastic face with too much ass fat in her blowfish lips. Garish makeup, ugly shoes. Very ugly shoes.

I wanted to kill her when she French kissed Sabrina's husband. I wanted to kill him when he grabbed her droopy butt and squeezed it. Hey, there were other guests in this hotel bar. We didn't come to watch some forty year old guy grope a fat lady like he was a drunken teenager.

Of course, that was exactly what I *had* come to see. So I took a few discreet photos and left.

When I showed the evidence to Sabrina, she didn't flinch. No tears. No wailing. She studied the eight by tens, then turned to me. "I wish he was dead."

"How much money do you have? I mean, how much can you get without drawing attention to yourself?"

We agreed on a price, and she stood up. "I need her. But I don't need him. I never did. I just didn't realize it until it was too late."

Sabrina was a strong woman. I'd have wanted to kill the rich bitch, too. Most women would have.

Six weeks later Sabrina's husband was in a scuba diving accident. He went down, down, down, and he never came up again.

A month after that, I received a package in the mail. A shoe box with the familiar logo for Miu Miu. The candy hots red went perfectly with a silk dress I bought on sale at the Rack.

****

As I made my way back to my car, my skin felt hot and tender to the touch. I'd look like cherries jubilee by nightfall. I knew what to do, though. Living in Florida with skin like mine, you learn what helps after the damage is done.

Nobody had ever seen me in my sunburn cure-all, my body gloppy with a thick white layer of Noxzema over a greasy coating of coconut oil. Nobody who wanted to live ever would.

And Ringo would have to keep his distance for at least twenty-four hours, maybe longer.

I speed-dialed him as soon as I reached the parking lot. I didn't bother to rinse my feet or change back into my clothes. While we talked, I hopped in the car and headed north. My news sucked, and he said so, but I had to agree Ringo's news sucked even more.

"Emworth's a liar. So's her driver. I went out there today. To her mansion in Orchid Breeze."

He paused for dramatic effect. I'd taught my assistant a thing or two, both inside and outside the bedroom. When I'd hired him, he'd been your typical tough guy, the big-strong-silent type. Now he could tell a story like your best girlfriend. I was proud of what I'd accomplished. Ringo would be able to please a woman now, make her happy as a female can get when she pairs up with a hunk of a man who communicates with juice and knows enough to add in the necessary details and delicious flourishes.

"Remember the Google map of her place? The big, long, majestic drive up through all them trees to the front?"

We always check out our clients who ask for special services. We conduct a thorough background search and monitor the movements of the client herself as well as her husband. No sense taking on a Mafia wife or someone lying just because they are in line to inherit a fortune. We need to trust our clients as much as they need to trust us. Ringo would be on Mrs. Emworth for the next week or two, gathering data, an essential part of the cooling off period.

"Sure, it was maybe a quarter mile loop," I answered.

I was on my way back to Deport Beach, crossing the short bridge over the inlet. But I was too distracted to appreciate the view. Usually I like watching all the million dollar yachts line up and wait for the drawbridge to rise so they can slide on past, gliding away to other worlds. Not today, though. I barely registered the turquoise beauty of the water below me as I chugged across.

"Okay, so you get the picture, Van. Me, sneaking up that long drive on foot, hoping nobody comes barreling down. It's hot today, too. I was sweating like a mutha."

I could picture it, all right. Ringo in his tight tee and floral board shorts, trying to be inconspicuous behind the twenty-foot hedge, surveying the multi-acre property. Holding binoculars to his piercing eyes while the perspiration dripped down the sides of his thick neck, gathering in the soft curls on his chest. Running from cocoplum to cabbage palm, his long hard legs flexing, his ass crack wet with sweat. He looked pretty damn sexy in my mind's eye, so I had to remind myself to remain professional.

"And?" I said in a curt voice.

"*And* I caught the two of them. Sitting together out on the wrap-around porch. Drinkin' coffee together. Mrs. Emworth and Jojo, her lying ass driver. The little fuckstick."

Google had some nice shots of that massive porch. The house was a new build in a hyperactive antebellum style. Huge white fans hung from the ceiling, and they'd positioned enough Southern rockers to amuse an entire nursing home. I pictured the scene in my mind. What I couldn't imagine was some young dude dressed in an oversize chauffeur's suit sharing a coffee break with his employer. Mrs. Emworth and her driver? No way.

"No way," I said.

"Yes way," Ringo corrected. "Weird, man. I watched them for a while. He kept taking phone calls. In front of her. Like that was okay."

He snorted. It was ridiculous. Rich people never sit around listening to their employees yak on the phone. This just isn't how it works. In Palm Beach, there's an unspoken division of classes. People like Jojo might have class, but to the top percenters, it's all low. That's how the moneyed see it. For the elite, the help is the help. They're not friends. They don't hang out. Never happens.

"He got a ton of calls. Seemed awful popular, for a cretin chauffeur."

Something was off. But what? I knew what my

assistant did next. He did what I would have done. "So you called him up."

"Yep. And he lied. Told me they were up on Worth Ave. Said she was shopping for clothes and getting waxed. Prepping for a trip she's going on with Mr. Emworth."

"What the fuck? What's he lying to you for?"

"I have no idea. But after we hung up, I heard *her* laugh. Loud and hard. Like she got a real kick out of it."

"That's fucked up," I said, and my assistant grunted. "Where're you now?" I asked him. I was twenty minutes from the office and would just make it in time for my noon appointment. I was worried I wouldn't have time to clean off the sand and change out of my beach gear. I needed Ringo to cover for me, just in case. "Can you delay my client in the lobby if I need you to?"

"No problem. I'm out front, waiting on you. I can do whatever. Let me know what you need."

What I needed were mojitos on an intravenous feed and a week in St. Bart's. But that wasn't what I'd get. Not by a long shot.

****

The coastal road traffic irked me to no end. What had seemed leisurely and pleasant a few hours before now tortured me in my angst to get back to the office. Overly long red lights, crawling rental cars steered by oldsters who could barely see above the dashboard, throngs of half-naked beachgoers jaywalking everywhere. Brightly garbed bicyclists weaving in and out of traffic, earning honks and cuss outs from my fellow drivers. Didn't anybody work? The trip home felt endless.

I hate nonprofessional behavior, and that includes tardiness. But there was nothing I could do. It was tourist season in South Florida, and the entire slow-moving world was down for the next two months. Running late would be everyone's problem until the snowbirds flew back to New York. Or whatever cold state they escaped from each year in favor of making our everyday lives deeply annoying.

When I parked in front of my office building and jumped out of the car, wolf whistles startled me out of my black mood. Nothing like a show of appreciation to make a woman smile. The guys in the empty lot clapped and hooted.

Somebody called out, "Now that's the way to win an argument." Whatever that meant.

I laughed and hurried across the street, greeting Ringo with a quick nod. He climbed out of his tinted black Escalade and gave me a weird look. He was trying not to ogle but was failing. I got defensive, but part of me felt flattered. The weak, girly part of me.

"I had to wear this to meet with the guy in Boca. I told you, he was out by the pool." I was irritated that I felt compelled to explain myself. Ringo ran around half dressed, and he didn't bother to discuss his choice of outfit. Right? "You got a problem with my undercover?"

"Objection. Badgering the witness." My assistant licked his glistening lips. He gave me the eye, then turned away. "You're late. Buzz me when you're ready for her to come up."

I brushed past him, and I could feel his eyes on me as I took the stairs two at a time. Just as the front door closed behind me, one of the lot squatters yelled, "Best in show."

Ringo growled. "Watch it, fella. She don't like to get harassed."

I zipped across the lobby and hustled up the stairs, shedding sand in a Hansel and Gretel trail.

Within five minutes, I'd buzzed Ringo. All cleaned up and professional again, I sat before my computer, scanning my next client's file. I had been fully prepared for the current situation, of course. I'd stashed a Donna Karan summer skirt and blouse in the coat closet, in case I needed to attend a spur of the moment meeting somewhere upscale. But in this instance, I wanted the silk against my skin. Putting my skinny jeans back on was out of the question. Tight clothing would've been way too painful on my blossoming sunburn.

Irish people are not genetically predisposed to beach-going. It doesn't take a sleuth to figure that one out. A more difficult puzzle—what the hell was I doing in this part of the world, where the sun was an enemy you could never escape? Was I so ridiculous I was actually waiting for my near-ex to magically return to his former princely self? The odds on that were the same as spotting Elvis or Michael Jackson at the local Denny's. Or me getting a deep, dark tan.

I was grateful to hear the click of heels approaching the office door. I needed to switch gears. I was berating myself, and my skin hurt.

The rapid, insistent knock had an impatient, entitled sound. Which perfectly matched my client's uptight, narcissistic personality. But I was glad it was time to let another woman talk about her man problems. This always helps me forget about my own.

I hurried to the door.

For more than a month, Mrs. Grady had been overpaying me. Her appointments with me were not normal ones. In fact, they seemed more like hundred dollar an hour scream therapy sessions. I suffered through our meetings while adamantly denying my ability to assist with her case. At each meeting, I would insist that Ex-Treme Measures could not help with her relationship issues.

Mrs. Grady was experiencing something stronger than TI. She suffered from PI, permanent insanity. Or, as my assistant liked to say, she was one of them scary bitches with a fatal agenda. Unfortunately, we'd worked with dozens of women like her. Rather, we'd refused to work for dozens of crazy, vindictive bitches like Mrs. Grady.

"I'm late because *this*," she said when I opened the door.

She posed for me, on display, small hip jutted to one side. She pointed one sharp finger at the constellation of brown stains on her white designer skirt. Coffee. Starbucks take-out, which appeared to have been ineffectively smudged with cold water. One of Ringo's favorite delay tactics.

"You should see guy who spill this on me," she added, after I'd moaned adequately and with the right amount of pity for her thousand dollar outfit. "He had body you die for."

No thanks. I'd rather enjoy it while I'm still alive.

Mrs. Grady stalked in and stomped around my office, staring at everything, seeing nothing. She did this every visit. I'd grown used to her hard-ass ADHD style. If she wanted to come here once a week and rant about her cheating husband, I'd continue to take her checks. But I refused to take her seriously.

"What you find this week? Have photos for me?" Her screechy voice pierced the soft quiet of the room. "I know he got girl. Least one girlfriend, the big fuck."

"I've had a man on Mr. Grady for sixty-two days in a row," I said.

This was an exaggeration. We'd backed off after the first few weeks. If he'd been dicking around, we would have known it. None of the telltale signs were there. His phone and email records were all accounted for, he hadn't slipped off anywhere, his home computer was clean. All the credit card bills lined up. Guy was straight as they come. Plus, he appeared to be devoted to his wife. Affectionate, generous, attentive. Watching them together had been unnerving. Especially since she was so hot to turn on him.

"Your husband has done absolutely nothing during these past eight weeks to indicate he's being unfaithful to you. So, no. I do not have any photos for you."

She stomped one tiny white Versace shoe. One of those sharp-heeled booties that run around twelve hundred dollars. Her dark eyes flashed in my direction, then away. When she opened her heavily lipsticked mouth to begin yelling at me, I put up a hand. No more. We'd already been through this several times too many.

"I understand how frustrated you must feel, Mrs. Grady. But he's going to work every day at the investment firm, then coming home to you. He just isn't up to anything, at least in the extramarital department. We've checked into his behavior at the office and, like I told you last time you were here, it's impeccable. We've captured every keystroke he makes on his office computer, listened to every phone call he's made. All that man does is work. And call home."

I softened my tone, appealing to her rational side. Like there was one. "You might want to confront your husband with your fears, address your concerns to him directly. I'm afraid we cannot be of much use to—"

"I know I right," she said, her small face reddening. "I his wife. You not. I need you do what I ask. You come high recommend. Your special services. He deserve to be punish. I can't believe you don't help me."

She tossed her waterfall of thick black hair. She would have been beautiful if she didn't make herself so ugly. I wasn't sure why she seemed to hate her husband so much, but I had a hunch it was because he was all that stood between her and his plucky investment portfolio.

I shook my head. "We're not in the punishment business, Mrs. Grady. We feel it is punishment enough to break up a marriage of long standing. When we provide the evidence to end a relationship, everyone suffers. Be grateful we have nothing like that for you."

She steamed over to the desk and stood too close to me, her ninety-five pounds of perfectly toned flesh trembling with frustration. Despite her ire, she smelled gorgeous, perfumed with the best scents available to those who can spend lavishly on their own aroma. She lasered into my tender skin with her hateful glare. *Ouch.*

This was a woman used to getting her own way. I think she might have slapped me if she didn't believe I was there to help her.

"I pay one more week. You not find husband in

compromising position by weekend, I file complaint. Report to Better Business Bureau. And attorney. You stealing from me, make promises you not fill."

"Are you threatening me?"

Now I stood up and moved closer, towering over the petite Asian shrew. I could wrap my hands around her twig-like neck and end this pointless discussion in less time than it took her to put on her eyeliner. She used way too much eyeliner anyway.

She flinched a little, as if slapped. I kept my tone steady and assertive. "Ex-Treme Measures is a highly regarded investigative agency. We have a reputation to uphold. I am always professional and law abiding. We do not participate in entrapment. Nor do we bend to idle threats."

She had nothing to say to that. Some of it was even true.

"Let me walk you to the door, Mrs. Grady."

She was just another spoiled mail-order bride. I wondered if she'd been a bitch before she arrived in the U.S. years ago or if her nasty personality was a learned trait. If it hadn't been so politically incorrect, I might have suggested she could go back to where she came from. But that might have been Hell, so I said nothing and herded her to the front door.

As she stepped out into the empty hall, she snarled. "So that it? No more watching husband?"

"That's it, Mrs. Grady. You're on your own. If I were you, I'd make him his favorite dinner tonight, then screw his brains out. You're the luckiest client to seek out my services in at least a year. Appreciate it."

I shut the door in her face. Gently, but firmly.

Other women would kill for a rich, faithful

husband like Mr. Grady. And that bitch wanted him killed? Was true love obsolete or what?

I sighed, returning to my desk. In the last couple decades, the reported incidence of adultery has gone up more than fifty percent. The majority of adulterers are men. It's always been this way. Some experts blame the Internet for easing the transition from curious to active cheating. But whenever I think about my own clients, I wonder whether the era of romantic love and long-term attachment is just plain over. If men don't need to mate for life, if their third party options are just a click away, why would they choose to settle down?

And with women like Mrs. Grady in the wife pool, was it any wonder?

I shook my curls, which had that been-to-the-beach frizz-bounce to them. I wasn't always sure where my loyalties lay. Sometimes I was on the wife's side. One hundred percent. But then I would work with a client who made me realize how difficult a relationship can be for the man. And the biological imperative couldn't be easy to ignore either.

I finished with Mrs. Grady's file and transferred it to the folder for former clients.

Chapter Eight

A few minutes later, Ringo interrupted my dull tour through solicitations, spam, and the weekly reminder for the upcoming Boston Latin high school reunion. Would I fly up there this summer to party with my former classmates? Would I show up at some swanky hotel and greet my old friends? I could picture it now— an air-conditioned ballroom with piped-in elevator music and rows of linen-covered tables. All those smug couples, a little fatter but a lot more self-satisfied, only too happy to brag about their PhD programs, their genius offspring, their tutors and nannies, vacation homes and world travels. What would I have to offer? An amusing anecdote about the time a body washed up on Hollywood Beach and the widow that almost killed me before I convinced her to calm the fuck down? How about if I shared blow by blow descriptions of the many ways one can dispose of an unwanted spouse without losing one's home and savings?

No, I had no interest in attending the class reunion. I had nothing to say to those people. Nothing I *could* say. Besides, I needed to stay away from my past. Unfortunately, I was beginning to fantasize about escaping from my present as well. But then, what would be left?

Ringo stood beside my desk, not saying anything for a minute. He was chuckling. At least one of us still had a sense of humor.

"That one's a piece of work. You like the abstract expressionism on that scary bitch's Snow White get-up?" he finally asked.

I guess he wanted my approval. "That's the last good latté you'll have to waste on her," I said.

He smirked. "Excellent. *Konnichiwa* to that bitch."

"Mrs. Grady is not Japanese. Duh. But you're right, she's history. As of five minutes ago, our contract with that particularly repellent client came to a blessed end. Thank god."

Ringo and I smiled at one another.

"Hey," he said, "glad you put an end to that trend. But right now, thanks to that evil PI, I need to caffeinate."

"I'll brew." I was better at making a heady cup of coffee, and we both knew it. "Tell me everything you saw out at Orchid Breeze. See if we can figure out the angle."

While I fiddled with the espresso machine, Ringo reported his findings in more detail. The intimacy between our client and her driver. How close they sat in their rockers. The way they huddled together after phone calls. The absence of other help, visitors, activity on the property. No sign of gardeners, pool cleaners, handymen, or maids. Highly unusual in that part of town.

He ended his monologue with a deep, rumbling sigh.

"What's that for?" I carried over the steaming cups of coffee.

He stood up to take the tray from me, setting it on the glass table. Such a gentleman.

"I dunno, Van. Things seem to be changing. You notice how most of our clients lately are either scammin', screamin', or lyin' about everything? When's the last time we got somebody in here who turned out to be straight up?"

I plopped down on the couch. "I know. I *so* thought Mrs. Emworth would work out for us. She seemed like the real deal. I'm in the mood for a good extermination. It's been months."

Ringo sipped and said, "Great coffee."

"Aren't you?"

"Aren't I what?" He sat back in the wing chair, overpowering it. He looked at me and shrugged his brows. "What?"

"Aren't you anxious to do a hit for a decent client? A good, solid gig? Where we can face down yet another of the world's millions of cheating scumbags and righteously remove one more from the pockmarked face of our troubled planet?"

I was only half kidding. Which half? Unknown.

Ringo stared deep in his coffee, avoiding my eyes. "Not really."

What? *"Not really?* What's that supposed to mean?"

The coffee was so hot, I burned the tip of my tongue. *Shit.* I have no idea how Ringo can drink anything that hot. The man's tough, inside and out.

For some reason, this thought made me want to feel his lips on the tops of my thighs. My hot pink thighs. I set my coffee down.

"I guess it means I think we should avoid makin' any hasty moves. I guess it means I'm afraid we need to rethink our professional goals." He paused. "You know how much I like workin' with you. Etcetera." He gave me one of those devoted puppy dog looks. "But I have an issue with the current business model."

This was news. "Really? Do tell," I said in a snotty tone.

"Vanna, come on. I'm not talkin' game here. Don't make this more difficult than it has to be. I'm being honest."

"Sorry," I said. *Mea culpa.*

After all, he had a valid point. Ex-Treme Measures had been more successful in the past. Maybe it was due to the recession, but lately our business had slacked off. The clients all required a lot of hand holding, and we'd ended up returning quite a few retainers. More often, our special services were either unwarranted or unwise. Now, with Emworth, Cantor, and Grady looking like strikeouts, we were in a bit of a slump.

"No hits, no errors," I said. "We have to play smart. So, yeah, three out of our last four clients haven't paid off. Not big, that is. But what's wrong with our business model? You have any ideas on that?"

He put his empty cup on the coffee table and rested his palms on his knees. His knees looked nice, smooth, and evenly tanned. I liked Ringo's knees. I liked his everything, actually.

"Our clients are some of the saddest people I ever met," my assistant said.

Of course they were. These women were losing the center of their life, their very reason for being. Of course they were *sad*. They were deeply depressed. Angry. Crazed. I wanted to say *duh*, again, but I just let him continue. Get it off his big, ripped chest.

"I mean, they're either fuming so much the friggin'

smoke is coming out their ears, or they're like fragile shells, all the meat sucked out of 'em. And lately, we been getting dangerous ones like Mrs. Grady and Mrs. Cantor. Maybe Mrs. Emworth, too. That bitch could be up to something that would cost us. Cost us everything."

He tilted his head, and we locked eyes.

"I'm here because of you, Van. I've stayed these past five years because of you. But I really think we should consider closing up shop. Relocating, before we end up becoming sad people, too. Or seriously depressed. Or worse. I mean, we could end up with a couple of steel-jacketed antidepressants to the back of the head."

I almost laughed. That was funny. But not really. Over the years, I'd entertained similar thoughts myself. But I had shared them with no one. Ringo was right. We were vulnerable. Vulnerable to the casualties of the trade. Vulnerable to burnout, shootout, attack, or arrest. And we could certainly go elsewhere, start clean, look for new clients. No sense ruining what we'd built or ending up in trouble by overstaying our welcome. He'd made a valid point. Now that the wrong kind of clients were hearing about us via the Richie Rich grapevine, maybe Ex-Treme Measures had too much transparency. Because who else knew about our special services? People like Brad Dickensen, that's who.

But relocate Ex-Treme Measures *now*? Relocate where? And what about my maybe-not-ex?

"Where did you have in mind?" I asked, finally able to sip a little of the super strong coffee without maiming myself. My mind raced ahead. Was Ringo threatening to leave? Would he go without me?

"Anywhere but here. Well, not really. But we've earned a reputation in Palm Beach and now it's biting us in the ass." He leaned back in the chair and stretched out his long legs. Sunlight from the lovely day outside the office windows lit up his choco-mocha tan. He looked good enough to dunk in my coffee and slurp.

"Emworth and her driver could be a couple of dirty blackmailers, Van. 'Course they might just be undercover agents trying to bring us down. Who the hell knows? That scary bitch Mrs. Cantor went and hired a hitman, one who banged her husband instead of doin' him. Now she's gotta walk the walk or they can haul her fat ass into the local cop shop."

He shook his head. Yeah, things sure were fucked up. But I liked hearing him talk the talk. I must admit, that kind of on the force, tough guy chatter really turned me on.

"Dickensen's running a nightmare version of Ex-Treme Measures and, by moving into our territory, he could easily blow our operation out of the water. We really should find out who the client is, whoever he's really working for. Whoever hired those pit bulls at Robes, Pierre. Could be Mafia, could be anybody. Probably nobody we wanna compete with." He sat forward, his face glum. "And now Grady's threatening to sue. We can't have that. We can't have none of this shit and still operate like we been."

Ringo stood up, staring down at me from his genetically predetermined, unfair advantage. He had me on height, strength, and masculine ego. His skin tanned easily, without pain or mottling, and he didn't have any estrogen to flood his brain when he was trying to make a decision. I wanted to jump up and kiss him. I wanted to throttle him and cry out, "Not fair!"

Instead, I crossed my legs carefully, which stung my thighs, and I said with a tight smile, "We still have Dominique Viscoti Premini, don't forget. And her gig is coming right up. This weekend, remember?"

Dominique Viscoti Premini had come to us via the recommendation of two satisfied clients, both of whom had been unhappily married socialites with much younger husbands. Cougars, in the parlance of our times. That is, older women who can afford to buy themselves young, pretty mates. In each case, the man stood to inherit massive wealth if anything were to happen to his aging wife. In each case, the husband soon strayed and found himself a lover, in both instances a hot young girl the age of our clients' granddaughters. One can understand why our clients were insulted, hurt, and embarrassed. One cannot understand why these women did not have prenuptial agreements. Anyway, once we did our research, we uncovered a history of indiscriminate unfaithfulness, ballsy embezzlement, and some horrific physical abuse, all issues the socialites did not want aired.

For each unhappy wife, Ex-Treme Measures took care of the problem, responding to the personal needs of the client. We were paid generously for our discretion and professionalism. Gigs like these made me proud of the services we offered our clients at Ex-Treme Measures.

But now I was forced to wonder if Ringo had gone along with these and other ex-terminations just to please me. Whenever we eased a cheating, lying, abusive parasite into an early grave, didn't he feel the emotional rush of vindication, the surge of adrenalin pumping through his body, the cooling of his hot blood pulse?

Maybe not.

"Van, I think we need to put a hold on Mrs. Premini's case. For security reasons."

He was pacing now, back and forth by my desk. He had his hands clasped behind his back, and his face was drawn tight. For the first time since I'd hired my assistant, he looked like a scared rabbit. An oversize, hunky-looking rabbit, but one that wanted to bolt.

"Ring, man, please calm down. We've had this thing lined up for weeks. It's all ready to go. We move on it on Saturday. We're in this one all the way, one hundred percent."

He kept pacing. And sweating. His tight tee stuck to his damp back. His eyes did not meet mine.

"Maybe you shouldn't have caffeinated," I said. "You're acting all angsty, like one of our clients."

I wasn't trying to insult him, just nudge him away from the precipice of a panic attack.

He turned on me, scowling. "Low blow. Uncalled for. For god's sake, Vanna. Do a review, girl. We're under threat from every side. The smart move would be to *not* move on this one. The smart move would be to fucken move *on*."

He walked over and stared down at me. I could see it in his face, like a big red tattoo across his handsome features. He loved me, so now he was afraid for me.

Shit.

Such emotions were no good. Not for Ex-Treme Measures, not for me and Ringo. Any kind of emotional attachment was unprofessional and would not be useful, considering the kind of business we were in. Love, in general, was bad for our business. Anger, distrust, a deep resentment toward the opposite sex were what had built Ex-Treme Measures. A buddy fuck and a sense of companionship, these indulgences hadn't interfered with our work. Animal magnetism and the sex that resulted, such things were totally understandable. Passion happens. But romance was out. No pair bonding. No, no, no.

"I got a wild hair this morning and made us reservations," Ringo said in a quiet voice.

He dropped to one knee before me, clasped my reddening thigh in his warm paw and looked me straight in the eye. His hand shook a little, but not as much as his voice when he said, "Please come to Auckland with me. I booked us on Qantas. We leave Saturday morning for LAX."

Holy shit.

I stared back at him, my sunburn screaming under the weight of his hand. I was trying to decide how to word my rejection. *Are you insane* was too harsh but accurate. Was he suffering from TI? Was I *that* good in bed last night? I couldn't ask him that. So I decided to focus on our work schedule and leave the romantic implications of his proposal for later.

"Objection. Baiting the witness," I joked. He didn't smile, so I said, "We'll have to return the retainer if we don't do the job for Mrs. Viscoti Premini. I don't want to have to do that. We won't earn out the money we got from Mrs. Emworth. That fee's going to go. Cantor and Grady are history. We'll never earn another cent from either of them."

I watched a drop of sweat drip off his long straight nose. A perfect nose. Very manly. I loved it when he snuffled me with that nose.

"Listen, Ring, I get what you're telling me." My tone was soft now. "But we need the money. *I* need the money. I need to finish paying off the creditors. For Ashton's last stint in rehab." Lame but true. "Can't you change the res? Delay the trip? So we have time to think this over, discuss it more?"

I was wheedling. I needed him on this one. I needed the job. Ex-Treme Measures needed the hit.

Ringo unclasped my throbbing thigh and stood. I could still feel his grip on my leg. Despite the pain it had caused, I missed his touch.

"I think this is where I say somethin' I didn't plan on saying. Somethin' I don't wanna say." He wandered to the window and took a deep breath. Sunlight bathed his skin, softening it to a golden bronze. "See, I'm gonna be on that plane, Van. I want to be with you, but I got to think about what's right for me, too." He turned again to face me, his dark eyes pleading. "We're too exposed. It's too dangerous and, I gotta say, I been finding our work problematic. It's like extremely unrewarding spiritually. I'd prefer to be doing something that makes us both happy. I don't want to stalk miserable marrieds anymore. I'm tired of knockin' off bad husbands. Too fucken depressing."

"You're monologuing, Ring." I was too surprised at his honesty to respond honestly. But I was thinking, *Now* the job dissatisfaction emerges? Why *now*? Why did he choose *this* moment to share his long-held grievances?

Men. They never talk about what's on their minds until the worst possible time.

He gave me a mean look. I scowled back. The

moment held, as if we were on the edge of something truthful. Truthful and dangerous.

"So you won't help me with the gig on Saturday?" Annoyance crept into my voice, but my anger was held in check by an overwhelming sense of disappointment. He was leaving, just like that? Wasn't he supposed to give me two weeks' notice?

"Sorry. As your security advisor, I suggest you postpone that job indefinitely. Come with me. Leave the country. Let's get away from these lunatic clients, their gay hitmen and suspicious drivers, the scary bitches with their ageless bodies and fatal agendas. Let's haul ass outta goofy South Florida. Let the crazy fuckers carry on without us."

I didn't know what to say, so I said nothing. I just sat there, sipping my cooling coffee. He watched me decide by not making a decision, then he nodded, the disappointment dark in his eyes.

My assistant straightened his wide shoulders, walked to the door, and opened it. He was leaving, all right.

"I'll send you an email with the flight info. I'm done here. I gotta go pack, deal with my landlord about breakin' the lease. Call me when you decide what you want to do."

He knew what I'd already decided. But he didn't look back. Ringo walked out the door, closing it firmly behind him.

I wanted to jump up and go after him. Grab him by the waist, yell a little, hug him, slap his sad face until he snapped out of it. I doubted he was strutting down the hall. He was slinking, dragging his sorry ass. I was sure he didn't feel very good about what he was doing. I was sure he didn't feel good about leaving me hanging.

In spite of that, the man was running. Away from me, our life here, Ex-Treme Measures.

And when I thought about it, I had to admit something to myself. In all honesty, I didn't blame him. He was being smart. I wasn't. I was the one behaving like a duh.

****

On Saturday afternoon, I sat on my front porch, talking to the guy who loved me most in the world. The one male who would never leave me, no matter how scared of the future he might be. No matter how mean I acted, how old I got, how fat or cranky I became. He was in it with me for the long haul. One hundred percent.

While I hand-fed my boy a sliced fig, I told him how much I appreciated his loyalty and support. "Popeye, you're the man. Twelve straight years of your undivided attention has made me the woman I am today. You go where I go. You're always there for me, hanging in whenever the road gets bumpy. Which it does, right? Life's like that, bumpy as hell. Am I right?"

Popeye watched me with one yellow eye and said nothing. He used to whistle a lot and say *hello baby* whenever he felt the urge to express. He had an extensive vocabulary and liked to show it off. He had always seemed like a happy guy. But that was before the female moved onto the next perch. Maybe agreeing to care for Porsche had been a terrible mistake on my part. Maybe I was a fucking ex-pert at making terrible mistakes.

"Porsche must be stupid or blind not to see you're

the best thing to come into her life since these organic figs from California." I sweet-talked my baby until he took the fruit sliver I offered him. He removed it gently from my fingers using his sharp black bill. "She's an idiot not to worship the birdshitty newspapers you walk on, Pops."

Speaking of idiots, by now I had to assume my unfaithful assistant had split on me. I pictured him aloft, squished into a narrow seat on a Southwest flight to Los Angeles. His plane had departed on time. I'd checked the status online. His flight from LAX to Auckland would depart in three hours.

"Ringo flew the coop," I told Popeye. "Do you believe that freaking guy?"

Popeye blinked one eye and turned away. He hated to see me get sentimental and squishy over some other male. I could tell.

But I wasn't feeling all that mushy. I had my own plans. By the time that particular male was making his way down the aisle of the Qantas plane to his seat in coach, I would be standing in Dominique Viscoti Premini's black marble master bath. I'd be dressed in black cotton with a color-coordinated nylon stocking mask, and I would be well hidden behind the black-and-white striped, double-sateen curtain of her steam shower room. This is where I would wait patiently for her young husband to come in from his daily workout.

This was my working plan, anyway. Fuck Ringo and his neurotic drive to escape all imagined threats. Life was full of threats. You can't just run away from them all. I would be okay without him. I would work the gigs solo, keep the business running by myself, and carry out the investigations, including our specialty services, on my own. I'd done it before I hired Ringo, hadn't I? So I could certainly function without his aid. After all, the last thing I needed was a fear-driven, love-addled assistant. Ex-Treme Measures would survive without him.

I didn't want to think about all the leg work he conducted so thoroughly, so efficiently. I didn't want to think about how big and strong he was, making our body disposal services possible. I didn't want to think about how I might need him in order to ex-ecute a successful ex-termination.

I especially didn't want to think about how I felt about him. About losing him. About wanting him back.

So I thought about work instead. While I was, as usual, not sleeping all night, I'd created an alternate plan for the upcoming gig, one I could work by myself. Several sleepless nights of planning and analysis had firmed up my POA.

Now I was good to go. Solo.

Good to go solo.

"Pops, I want you to give me a widdle kiss."

I suckled a thick slice of fig and reached for my parrot. If I held him up to my face, he would lean in and take the bite of fruit from between my lips. Our special smooch.

"I want your wuv," I said to my feathery baby.

Porsche fluffed her sleek feathers on the next perch, ignoring us. She'd been preening herself, occasionally looking up to watch puffy clouds scuttle across the pale blue sky. She'd eaten her rice cake crumbs with an air of disdain. What a snobby bitch. As always, she seemed unreachable. Parrots tend to bond tight with their first owner, then refuse to connect with all others. So I was ignoring her, too.

The minute I brought Popeye toward my face, there was a sudden flurry of wings.

Ouch. Fuck!

I instantly let go of the bird. The squawking was deafening and in stereo. I covered my ears and watched as both parrots swooped around the porch, screaming at one another. My bottom lip stung. I licked at it, tasting blood.

"Evil bitch," I mumbled as I covered my bleeding mouth with one hand, my head with the other.

The parrots squawked and fluttered about. I hurried inside the house, slamming the door behind me, hoping they would calm down and stop the eardrum-shattering noise. My pink sweatshirt was splattered with blood.

"Fucking just what I need," I stuttered as I hurried into the bathroom for something to staunch the flow. Porsche must have thought I was a threat. And, like so many females, she'd only discovered her desire for a male once she thought somebody else wanted him. So she'd attacked the competition—me.

Two blood-soaked hand towels later, I bandaged my lip as best I could. I'd have to head for the closest doc-in-a-box. I needed stitches, and I needed them quick. I fantasized about not feeding Ms. Sharp Beak for a couple of weeks, putting her on the *fuck you* diet. But when I stepped out onto the silent porch, I quickly changed my mind.

The two Greys sat together on Popeye's perch. They huddled close, preening one another. I had to smile, which made my lip bleed more. Nature was harsh, difficult, and just a little too predictable.

I started up the car and backed out while pressing a

bloody facecloth to my mouth. How long would the birds' love-fest last? African Greys are one of those species that supposedly mate for life. Ha. I'd believe that if I saw it firsthand.

My sneering cynicism made my lip bleed even more.

The drive was maddeningly slow. I tried not to drip onto the crackled vinyl seats of my VW. I'm sure I looked like a war refugee, with my hair unbrushed, my shirt bloodstained, a blood-soaked cloth gritted between my coffee-stained teeth.

As I rolled into town, I found myself thinking about Ringo. It would've been so great if I could've called him, told him about the birds. Whined about my injury. Laughed with him a little bit. But I couldn't call him. Not now. No way. So I felt pretty goddam sorry for myself. For whatever reason, I'd chosen loyalty to my ex and devotion to my clients over my bonds of friendship and trust with Ringo.

My former assistant must have mulled over the implications of that choice already. He must have felt hurt by my decision. *Ouch.*

But he'd be fine. He'd bounce back fast. A good-looking young guy like Ringo could have a new woman in his bed before the sun set on the southern hemisphere.

I frowned until blood spurted from my punctured lip and splattered on the steering wheel. *Shit.*

The lot for the strip mall was blissfully uncrowded. I pulled up in front of a neon sign for the Emergen-C clinic and parked. Then I turned off my phone, in case I was tempted to call Ringo when I saw the needle and the surgical thread. I had to buck up, take my stitches like a man.

Holding the soaked rag to my mouth, I hustled inside the doc box. I tried to convince myself that not talking was my best move. Talking to Ringo would make my lip hurt. Hearing his voice might even make me cry.

Chapter Nine

A few hours later, I got ready to go to the gig at Mrs. Viscoti Premini's. But my plans were spoiled when I couldn't dress in my camo gear. The spot where I now had nineteen very sore stitches rubbed against the nylon mask, so I took it off. There was no way I'd be able to wear something over my face, not now. And my tight black turtleneck was out of the question, I couldn't even get the shirt over my head without endangering my fat and tender lip.

When I talked, it sounded like I had a mouth full of grapes.

I wasn't one for pain meds. I preferred my numbness from a bottle or a frosted mug. But the throb in my lip was incessant. And distracting, which could be dangerous while I was on the job. So, after I carefully dressed in my darkest but loosest long-sleeved T-shirt and sweats, I took a few teeny sips of the liquid pain medication I planned to use for the job. Then I popped two of the antibiotic capsules the doctor had prescribed.

The on-duty doc-in-the-box turned out to be a bespectacled girl who didn't seem old enough to drive, never mind sew up my face. Between stitches, she advised me to watch out for infection. She also warned me not to get too close to the mating birds. Like I didn't get that already.

I'd been badly humiliated, wounded, and stitched together by a teenager. Still, I refused to let a little pet-related injury dampen my spirits. Now I was ready to ex-terminate a bad husband for a good client. One hundred percent ready.

On my way out the front door, I gave the two love birds a wide berth. Their cooing happiness really pissed me off. When I mumbled, "Fuck you, bitch. And you, too, traitor," neither one looked up from their mutual grooming. Was he fondling her feathers?

"Maybe you two should take this to a hotel," I suggested, but they didn't respond. Maybe because everything I said came out sounding like *thoot, thoot.* Like pebbles shot through a straw.

I left the top down on my car and started her up. Even though a slapping wind was probably not the best thing for my wound, the cool air would feel good on my face. Plus, I felt a tiny bit sleepy, the way you do after a doctor's appointment. After a traumatic injury. After your own beloved attacks you and draws blood. Anyway, I needed the fresh air. And I wasn't bleeding anymore. The weensie sips of pain med had made all my muscles relax. The thrumming on my face had receded. My sunburn still stung, though. And a glance in the rearview mirror confirmed it. I looked like hell.

The evening was overcast and a bit chilly, and the traffic was subdued in response. This cheered me. In fact, I felt better than I had all day. I eased the car through town and, under all the ruined skin, the lip gash, the stitches, I felt pretty damn good. If it hadn't been a threat to my wound, I might've smiled. No wonder Ashton was a drug addict. Half a hit of this pain shit, Dilaudid, and my world had markedly improved.

The near-instant reduction in physical and psychic pain was like sex. It takes you out of yourself, leaving all your bad shit behind.

Which was what I'd needed right at that moment. No past, no worries about the future, nothing but me, right here, right now, feeling good.

When I reached A1A, I took a left and headed north. On my right, the restless ocean washed ashore in ragged waves, scratching at the narrow strip of sand. High tide has become a scary reminder of what global warming is doing to our planet. Severe erosion has chopped up our beaches. Every year the shoreline lessens as the sea takes bigger and bigger bites. Each winter, the water seems to get a better purchase on the beach. With each summer hurricane, the shoreline diminishes even more. Soon enough, the beachfront mansions will have saltwater swimming pools. Then they'll *be* saltwater pools.

But as I hummed along the scenic route to the Viscoti Premini estate, I wasn't in the mood to dwell on the negative. My heart wasn't bleeding for the one percent and their second homes facing an overheated Atlantic Ocean. I didn't want to worry about the shrinking polar icecaps, the rising seas threatening the rest of us, too. On my way to the gig, I needed to remain cold, clear, and empty. Like a glass of Stoli, looking like nothing but packing a delightful wallop.

Dominique Viscoti Premini had come to us prepared to do what it takes to remove a bloodsucking leech from her Botox-infused, salon-tanned, surgically resurfaced flesh. I was flattered to get her business. The woman was a local legend. She practically ruled Worth Avenue, invading the luxe shops on a daily basis, entourage in tow. The clerks had nicknamed her Queen Worth. In a town like Palm Beach, where everybody acts like the latest Mrs. Donald Trump, Mrs. Viscoti Premini had a lot of stiff—and I do mean stiff, as in plasticized almost to *rigor mortis*—competition. Still, she was renowned for her severe case of situational entitlement. As Ringo would say, the scary bitch was a real piece of work.

He didn't like her. But Ringo didn't like most of our clients. He was intimidated by the angry wives, disgusted by the gold-diggers. I had more tolerance than my assistant, but I didn't like Mrs. Viscoti Premini very much, either. Too rich from ex-husbands' estates, too dismissive of those who earned their money the hard way.

But, I had to admit, she had a legitimate case. Barely out of a training bra, she'd married up. Over the years that followed, she'd established herself as a successful serial wife of glittering financial wizards. Then, approaching seventy and rolling in annuities and real estate, Queen Worth faltered. She fell for a younger man. A much younger man.

The new husband, Tristan, was a hot and sexy mistake. A thirty year old gigolo, the guy did nothing but shop on her dime, work out, and hunt for poontang.

My personal feelings about the client were unimportant. A week of investigation had proved, without a doubt, the husband was bad news, and the client had followed through as advised. Mrs. Viscoti Premini had done everything right—paid me in advance, awaited the required cooling off period, then said the magic words "I'm one hundred percent sure. I want that man dead."

And here I was, on assignment. Alone.

By the time I reached the southern tip of Palm Beach, it was dark. The moon hung overhead in an upside down smile. I smiled in response. Despite the stitched lip and the desertion of my assistant and lover—a seriously great lover, alas—I felt upbeat. Maybe it was the opioid talking, but I was looking forward to the night ahead of me. I knew I would feel good about two things—my skills as a problem solver for betrayed women and the rehab of my poor credit rating. Queen Worth may have been a bitch on limo wheels, but her retainer would relieve me of the last of the debt my soon-to-be ex had saddled me with. I was so ready to run free of that responsibility.

Run to where, I wasn't sure. But maybe this would be a good time to file for divorce. And rethink my life.

At least, that was what I was thinking when my phone rang. My heart sped up, but the caller wasn't Ringo.

"You said to call you if I needed to talk," the caller said, "but I'd rather come in. Can you see me tonight?"

"I've got business tonight," I told Mrs. Emworth. "How's Monday at noon?"

"What? You sound like you have something in your mouth. Are you having dinner? Where are you? Downtown? Can I come meet you?"

These rich bitches, they all assume if you're eating, you're in a nice restaurant. They all think they can impose on you just because they're paying you to do a job they don't want to do themselves.

No, I wasn't eating, and no, she couldn't meet me.

I repeated myself, speaking as slowly and clearly as possible through a lip the size of my thumb. What part of no would she not understand?

All of it.

She cut me off mid-*thoot*. "It's almost six now. I'm at the salon, but I'll be done here in a couple hours. I'll drop by your office on the way home." She hung up.

"No." I said it ten times in a row, but every time it sounded a lot like *okay*.

Shit.

Where was Ringo when I needed him? Oh, yeah, running away. Without me. *From* me, actually.

My high sank a little, but I managed to pump it up by boosting my Lady Gaga CD to top volume. I didn't eject the disc until I hit the traffic circle a mile from the client's estate. I needed to reduce my visibility at this point, slip into town unnoticed. Not an easy task when one is sporting a mangled lip while driving a convertible hippie car.

Just north of the circle, I pulled into the vast lot for a private country club. Mercedes and BMWs, Jags and classic Cadillacs were lined up like shiny new dimes on a platter, each one brighter than the next. I shaded my eyes from the auto bling.

Time to man my cover.

When I climbed out of the car, my legs felt strange, a bit wobbly. I limped back and popped the trunk. Then I pawed through the magnetic signage I carried with me. There were several possibilities that would work well in this neighborhood, but I went with Home Séances: www.doortodoorghosts.com. After all, I looked the part—half lunatic, half gypsy. Before one of the tony club valets could venture my way to harass me with their no trespassing bullshit, I stuck the sign on the driver's side door and jumped back in the car. I chugged over to the exit, escaping without making a scene.

Due to my new identity as a medium who makes house calls, the appropriateness of my presence in the land of luxury would not be questioned. As long as it appeared I was providing a service, no matter how ludicrous, I would have what looked like a valid reason to be visiting any number of private estates. Services were what kept the one percent running. These people didn't do much of anything for themselves. Put most of them on an uninhabited island and they'd be dead in a week.

For a minute, I considered ordering a new sign for my collection. What about www.yourasswiped.com? I had to force myself to stop laughing when I felt my stitches pulling.

I checked my phone, then shut it off. Mrs. Viscoti Premini had been informed she could cancel her contract up until the last minute. But that minute had passed at six p.m.

I always instruct my clients to make absolutely certain they wish to go through with our arrangement. Most of them find that they do. One of my clients, however, chickened out right before we went in. A battered wife from Lighthouse Point, she freaked at the starting gate and called us off. She just couldn't live with it, was what she'd said in a voice wracked with guilt. I told her I understood and returned three-quarters of her retainer. When she rehired us a year later, her face significantly scarred and her mojo no longer running on guilty, I was happy to provide her with the repeat client discount.

Once the phone was off, the gig was on. Queen

Worth had already left town, taking along her entourage. She was busy establishing her alibi for the time of death. If Tristan stuck to his normal routine, he would be the only one home. That is, until I arrived.

The Viscoti Premini estate sat up on a hill on several plush acres sandwiched between the Intracoastal and the Atlantic. The sand-colored mansion perched above Ocean Drive like a lioness, ready to spring at any moment and rip some poor animal's throat open. The late Mr. Viscoti, my client's first husband and the original contributor to her massive fortune, was a classic car buff and an art collector. In the back yard, he'd erected a huge garage for storing his several dozen antique cars. Upstairs from the cars, in a penile-shaped tower, he'd amassed a gallery of artwork by some of the world's most overpriced masters.

The idea of a private museum depressed me. Our investigations indicated there was a Shelby Cobra circa 1963—*wowza*—and a Tucker sedan, possibly the one they said burned up in a garage in Deland. We're talking amazing cars here, one of a kinds. On the walls up in the tower, sketches by Gauguin and Van Gogh, a Keith Haring, a small oil of a vaginal flower by none other than Georgia O'Keeffe. All this beauty stashed away in a rich man's playhouse, off-limits to the rest of us. Yes, we peons were prohibited from appreciating such priceless works of art. Like we were just too economically deprived to understand style and substance, the inherent value of the world's creative genius.

Mr. Viscoti's private museum represented the kind of hoarding we are taught as children not to indulge. He was like one of the kids who wouldn't share toys on the playground. Such a childish greed.

If I pulled in behind the garage, my car would be out of sight from both the road and the main house. Mrs.Viscoti Premini had dismantled the automatic lighting from the tower garage to ensure my vehicle would not be seen from the Intracoastal Waterway. No need to show off my presence to the evening booze cruises that regularly passed by.

The electronic gates were open as promised, so I pulled up the drive and rolled around back. I snugged the car up close to the tower to take advantage of the shadows it cast. Then I sat for a moment in the breezy, damp night air, reviewing the ex-termination plan in my mind.

When I went in on a gig, Ringo waited outside. My assistant kept close watch in case anything unexpected arose. Then, once I buzzed his cell, he would come help me with the heavy lifting. Pulling off a hit alone was definitely more of a risk.

But I'd started Ex-Treme Measures by myself, conducting all the early work on my own. I was not going to let my recent dependence on a man ruin my confidence. Not today. I had to make this happen so I could pay off my debts. And prove something to myself as well.

I took a deep breath while I fiddled with a dark green scarf I'd dug out of a lingerie drawer. I draped the silk over my head and around my hair, allowing some of the material to hang in my face. I could see through it, but not that clearly. I'd have to be careful not to trip. This was the best I could do since using my usual mask was out.

Next, I pulled on a pair of latex gloves, then added

elastic bands to my wrists and ankles. I encased myself in my clothing so that no hair or skin flakes could escape. That's all I needed, for some CSI lab to discover I'd been hanging in Queen Worth's bathroom.

Sitting in the car outside the Viscoti Premini estate, wrapped in green silk, rubber bands, and latex, I was almost ready to launch. My mind, however, hopped around like a Mexican jumping bean. I took several deep breaths and closed my eyes.

Simple breathing exercises usually helped to ease me into the empty space required to clear my head for the task at hand. I'd been practicing brief meditations before hits for years. But this time when I closed my eyes, I was so relaxed that I nodded off. Snore.

Holy shit.

I inhaled deeply, pinching my forearms as hard as I could while letting my breath out slowly. What the hell was wrong with me? I shook my head, grabbed my leather satchel and tossed it over one shoulder. Then I eased open the car door without making a sound. Ready or not, it was time to ex-terminate.

When I climbed out, my legs wobbled back and forth, finally folding up under me. I found myself squatting by the front end of my car, not sure how I got there. Then I remembered. Dilaudid. This narcotic analgesic was so much stronger than I'd imagined. How did my ex function, taking shit like this every day?

Oh, yeah, that's right. He didn't. The guy couldn't function *because* he was on these kinds of drugs. Neither, it appeared, could I. For some reason, this made me laugh. I giggled into my hand, and yes, this hurt my lip.

The sweet smell of night-blooming jasmine wafted

my way. I closed my eyes for a minute, floating on the delicious scent. I had to admit, the high felt great, all my senses so easily satisfied. And the world seemed nicer because I felt so warm inside. If I didn't have to do things like work and think clearly, I might want to recapture the feeling this drug gave me. Like every time I felt bad. Or needed to relax. Or wanted to sleep.

I had to jerk myself awake again. I was kind of out of it, and that wasn't so good. Especially since I didn't seem to give a shit. No wonder America was crawling with addicts. This stuff was the perfect antidote to our stressful, fucked up lives.

It wasn't easy to stand up. Wavy lines passed in front of my eyes, and when I took a few steps, it was a lot like walking a gangplank. Which should have freaked me out but made me want to laugh instead. I couldn't help it. I started snickering. My body was misbehaving, and I wasn't too sure about how well my brain was working. What a fool I was. Yet I felt good about that, too.

Even though I knew it was crazy to continue with the ex-termination plan, I did it anyway. So much for my judgment. I eased out from behind the car and crouched low for a scurry across the back lawn to the main house.

Sure, going forward with the hit was totally nuts. But wasn't killing off bad husbands insane anyway? Even though I was as high as my ditz-brained almost-ex, I knew the answer to that self-imposed question. Yes indeed, Ex-Treme Measures was absolute madness.

Low to the ground, I moved out. Around the side of the tower, down behind thick, jasmine-laced hedges, over to the flagstone path.

Then I saw him. Mrs. Viscoti Premini's cheating husband was out on the tennis court. I could hear the *thwack, thwack* of the ball and the *boing* of the automated server, the deep grunts as Tristan dove and reached.

We'd watched our boy long enough to know his routine. He exercised in the early evening, once his full day of shopping and preening and granting sexual favors was complete. On Saturdays, he spent an hour out on the halide-brightened grass court, hitting three hundred serves from the Wilson tennis ball machine. Then he did fifty laps in the illuminated, heated, Olympic-size pool. After that, he'd head for the master bath.

Which was where I would be waiting for him.

I had keys. I had the alarm code. I had a map of the eleven thousand square foot home, memorized from extensive blueprints. I knew he would take a long hot bath while sipping a nice cold St. Pauli Girl straight from the bottle. I knew where the cold drinks were kept, and I had my own bottle of carefully doctored beer with me. As I snuck up the back walkway to the servant's entrance, I checked my shoulder bag. The bottle was in there, but it had warmed. It would need to be chilled or he might reject it. I had to get it inside the mini-fridge in a hurry.

Unfortunately, my body seemed to be moving like I was underwater. In fact, I kind of felt like I was drowning in something. My breathing had slowed, and I could hear it. It sounded thick, somewhat labored.

The offshore breeze whacked me in the face as I fumbled around for the house keys my client had provided. The scarf felt damp and clingy but remained in place. At the back door, I struggled first with the lock, then the burglar alarm. The code fuzzed around my brain until I snatched it out of the floral night air and punched it in. I'd done this so many times with other clients I was operating on autopilot. Drug-addled autopilot in this case, but it worked.

The back hall was dark. I bumped up against the walls a few times and continued on my way, trying not to laugh. At myself, at the situation, at the plan to knock out some guy while he lounged in a gilded bathtub, then hold his head under the soapy water until he drowned. So silly, when all his mean old wife needed to do was toss him out on the street. Where she'd found him. Where he belonged.

I took the thickly carpeted back stairs to the second floor, and it wasn't easy. My legs each weighed an extra five pounds. Plus, everything around me seemed to be floating in a green mist. I had to force myself not to grab onto the polished wood of the balustrade, not to stroke the oil paintings of yachts and dancers adorning the walls or the busts of cowboys and presidents and cowboy presidents that stood on wrought-iron pedestals in the stairwell.

At the top of the stairs, I stopped to inhale the wondrous aroma of real leather, old dust, and excess money. Wow. Queen Worth sure lived in a sensory palace. Too bad she couldn't just sit back and enjoy it. Not let some stupid man ruin her fun.

Infants have infancy, adults have adultery. I don't know where I'd heard that line, but there in the Viscoti Premini estate, it popped into my mind. In light of the effort I was making, it struck me as hilarious. I laughed out loud, then stumbled down the hall.

I staggered into the master bedroom. The anti-glare lighting from the tennis court seeped into the room, brightening everything. I lifted my scarf and stared. It was like being inside a sunflower. Yellow. Yellow everywhere—wallpaper, thick brocade drapes, dozens of throw pillows, fluffy quilt on the king-size bed. I felt jaundiced. Who could look good in a room like this? Maybe a banana, certainly not a naked woman. Perhaps Mrs. Viscoti Premini needed an interior decorator instead of a hitman.

Hitwoman. Hitperson.

I was losing it. I wanted to lie down on the sunflower bed and close my tired eyes. I wanted to call Ringo and tell him to hold the plane, I'd changed my mind. Couldn't I change my mind, change my life? Couldn't I do something else with my mind, with my life?

Anything but this.

I staggered toward the master bath, but I was losing steam. I was tired, so tired. Why was I the one still in the trenches, trying to wage a private war on bad husbands?

No light pierced the glass block walls. A dark cavern the size of my office, the bathroom boasted a walk-in shower, separate toilet stalls—his and hers, of course, complete with their own marble sinks—a mirrored vanity that ran the length of one twenty-foot wall, and a massive, gold-flecked Jacuzzi tub.

I hurried over to the stainless steel fridge tucked under the vanity. The shelves had been cleared. Thank you, Mrs. Viscoti Premini. I set my special services beer bottle on the top row, front and center. Then I ducked into the steam room, complete with multiple shower heads and Bose stereo speakers built into the ceiling. I hid myself behind the heavy curtain separating the shower area from the rest of the bathroom.

Everything was in place. Me, the drink, the tub, the deserted house, the wife in Aspen with her witnesses. The beer had been updated with a generous amount of oral hydromorphone hydrochloride, mildly flavored with artificial sweeteners. Making a nice blend with the naturally hoppy German beer. If all went according to plan, Tristan would consume a more significant dose of Dilaudid than I had, and he'd experience a more significant high. Especially since he'd consume it in combination with alcohol. Oh, yes, Mr. Queen Worth would be feeling good fast. After drinking some of the special beer, bad hubby would be super relaxed, dazed and confused. And ready for me.

Unfortunately, I didn't feel so ready for him. I wasn't up for much, actually. My head spun, whirling and tilting and so light it seemed to float above me, up by the speakers. My skin felt clammy, yet I was still warm, a little sweaty. I leaned hard against the Italian marble tile wall, gradually sinking into a low squat. I'd organized the plan just as I always did, and it was unfolding so perfectly. All I had to do was relax into it. Like I always did on an ex-termination gig.

I closed my eyes. Oh, yes, I was relaxed all right. *Too* relaxed. I was so freaking relaxed I was lighter than air. I was flying. Way, way too high.

Chapter Ten

Okay, so I'd noticed the changes. In my behavior, in my attitude, in my enthusiasm for the work. And, yes, I had truly believed all those bad husbands deserved what I gave them. But the question haunting me was this. Was *I* the one to give it to them?

Suddenly, it seemed like I wasn't so sure.

The Jarwelli case the previous summer had shaken my confidence. Perhaps I was still reeling from that clusterfuck of a situation. Which could help to explain the situation I was in now.

Mrs. Jarwelli didn't make an appointment. She waited for me to arrive that morning, standing by herself on the front stoop outside my office building. Nobody hangs around out there, not if they don't want to get messed with. I thought she was a panhandler. I had my hand in my shoulder bag already, reaching for some loose change.

"Ms. Treme?" she asked in the gravel voice of a chain smoker. "May I speak with you?"

I nodded. "Shoot."

How prescient of me.

"I need some serious measures taken against a man," she said with a lilt in her tone. I didn't recognize it. Not Jamaican, not Haitian. Honduran?

After Mrs. Jarwelli explained that she knew a former client, I asked her to follow me inside. I led her to my office. She huffed pretty good, like those cigarettes had taken their toll. Her stooped posture and weathered face also contributed to the appearance of a very old woman.

Once we were seated and I'd fetched her a glass of spring water, Mrs. Jarwelli told me her story. As I listened my gut began to ache. It felt like I'd swallowed battery acid. I would have to lay off the espresso.

Our mutual acquaintance was a satisfied and wealthy client. But Mrs. Jarwelli was not and neither was her husband. They lived in the periphery of wealth, like most of us do. The couple worked for a family of gazillionaires. He captained the fleet of recreational water vehicles. A yacht, sailboats, a cigarette boat, jet skis, and the like. While she took care of the house. The laundry, the floors, the dusting and vacuuming. They both polished the silver and ran small errands.

"Which is how I know what the boss is up to," she said with a deep frown. "He's a Satanist. He worships the devil and needs to be stabbed through the heart with a stake."

"I think you have your ghouls mixed up. Satanists are not vampires. Usually." Actually, I was out of my depth. Bad husbands were my forte, not paranormal freaks. "What is the man doing that gives you the impression he is a Satan worshipper?"

I could only imagine. Maybe not.

"When the missus was out of town visiting her brother, the boss had a dark party at the house. That's what they call it, a dark party. He invited ten of his Satanist friends. They had sex on the garage floor and out in the boats. There was…stuff everywhere. My husband was horrified. He did not want to take the blame for the mess. I had to help him clean up before the missus came home." She shook her head, a look of disgust on her dried apple face. "And after that, since he knew we knew, he began sending us to the voodoo store. To purchase his artifacts." She shivered. "The missus is a good woman. Christian and pious. If she learned about all this, it would kill her."

She gave me the look. I could see it in her eyes. She wanted the bad husband dead so the good wife would be spared. And she wanted me to take care of it.

When she saw that I knew what she was asking, she removed an envelope from her threadbare cloth purse. She handed it to me. "A down payment. A retainer."

I agreed to look into the situation. I did not agree to make it go away. "I will need to see what your boss is up to, then we can decide what would be the best route to take."

After she left, I opened the envelope. It was coffee stained and smelled like smoke. Ten crisp hundred dollar bills. The woman wasn't kidding.

When I shared the lowdown with Ringo, he said he would put a watch on the estate. A few days later, he called in a report. "Rubber money," he told me. "They're rolling in it."

Funny.

"There's nothing suspicious going on, though," he said. "The wife, she's quite the hot number. Wouldn't be surprised if she wasn't up to tricks. But they seem pretty tame. Nothin' out of the ordinary. They're affectionate. And their lifestyle's quiet."

"What about him?" I asked.

"Nice looking guy in his sixties. Thick head of

hair, trim. Jogs, plays squash and golf. Drives an early Tesla that's worth a fortune. Talks on the phone to his cronies, but not about Satan."

"Well, keep on it. If there's a crack there, we need to find it. Otherwise, I'll give the deposit back. She should just go find another job. I don't think this one's our business. And I doubt she can pay for ex-treme measures anyway."

Ringo laughed. "Give the money back? This early? What's with you?"

"I lack confidence in this one."

Ringo whistled. "Wow. That doesn't sound like you."

It didn't. But neither did the case. The proposed hit was not on the client's dirty husband. It wasn't the client's dirty business. So why was it mine?

The next night as I was locking up, Ringo appeared in the hall behind me. He pushed by and sank onto the couch with a deep sigh.

I stared at him. "I hope this isn't going to take long. I'm ready for a hot shower and a cold drink. Not a boring client update." I rolled my eyes and put hand to hip. Gave him all the hurry up signals I knew.

He looked up at me. "We are not gettin' involved with this dude. You tell Mrs. Jarwelli to pass out her resume and find a new job. Her boss isn't a Satanist. He's a witch doctor."

I laughed. "A witch doctor? On the island? Married to a plastic Barbie? I don't think so."

Ringo shrugged. "Believe what you want to, Van. I saw it with my own eyes. He sends her to the voodoo store down in Homestead for candles and dried plants and little animal bones, shit like that. Then he builds a fire in the side yard while his wife is at the hairdresser. Throws shit in it, stands over it, and chants and stuff. I saw him, I heard him. He's putting a spell on somebody. And I sure don't want him to do it to us."

I shrugged and turned to leave. This was nonsense. I would take on cases of wife beaters, wife cheaters, perverts, and pedophiles. But people who practice a little paganism here and there? Not for me.

"This is pure crap," I told Ringo. "I'm going home. And you are officially off the case."

He grinned. "Thank god."

The next morning when I pulled up in front of the office, Mrs. Jarwelli was waiting for me again. I had been feeling nice and chippy after a hard five mile run on the beach, but my mood sank when I spotted her. I hated to let her down. She looked like she'd been let down way too many times in her life.

I locked my car and greeted her on the steps. Then I handed her the envelope with all her money still in it. I wasn't going to take her cash. Not if I couldn't help her. And I couldn't.

She nodded, her eyes dark and knowing. "He put you in a trance and tricked you into refusing my case. I have seen this kind of thing before," she told me in a charred whisper. "I hope nothing bad happens to you now. I am sorry I brought such evil into your life."

I shrugged. "You didn't bring me anything that hasn't already been there. I've been dealing with bad men all my life, Mrs. Jarwelli. You take care."

I went inside the building and left her standing there.

At the end of the day, Ringo called me from the Tam. "You see the four o'clock news?" he slurred.

"No. Why?"

I wanted a cold one so bad I could taste the foam. But a beer with Ringo was foreplay and I wasn't sure I was in the mood for that.

"Your Mrs. Jarwelli got arrested. She shot her employer. At close range. He's dead."

"Shit. No! What the hell was she thinking?"

"She told the wife she was ridding the world of evil. The wife beat her senseless with a candlestick, I guess. Then called the cops." He whistled. "What a mess."

I agreed. After I hung up, I noticed I was shaking. I hadn't helped that client by taking her on. I hadn't helped her by letting her go.

So what exactly *was* I doing?

****

I was still in the shower stall, cold and sleepy, weak. Ringo was shaking me by the shoulders, hard, and yelling in my face. "No more bad husband blood, Vanna!" His breath was warm and smelled like cinnamon coffee.

When I collapsed against him, he hugged me close, cradling my head to his chest. He started whispering in my ear, but I could barely hear him over the stringed lullaby of vaguely familiar classical music.

"One hundred percent chill," I thought he said. "No more scary bitches."

When I opened my eyes, I was alone. I was squatting in the shower stall, alone. My legs were numb, and I had cramps in my butt cheeks.

Gentle music drifted through the room, Beethoven or Brahms, I wasn't sure. I'm pretty ignorant when it comes to classical shit. I remained frozen in my painful squat, listening for the sound of someone splashing in the bath.

Except for the music, the room was silent. I tried not to freak out. How long had I slept? Had I missed my chance to pull off the hit? Was I totally fucked?

Then I heard him come in. Tristan, the bad husband, was whistling tunelessly, padding around on the marble floor. He opened the fridge and slammed it shut. A bottle cap popped.

Beer should have splashed down the side of a fluted glass next. That was the routine. He liked to luxuriate in his bath, sipping beer while soaking his hard-worked muscles in a bubbly froth of steaming hot water. I eased up into a crouch, listening, ready to spring into action.

I froze when I heard it. *Glug glug*. The familiar sound of beer being chugged.

Shit.

This was not part of the plan. Why wasn't he stretched out in the tub, sipping his beer slowly from a crystal glass? Why had he chug-a-lugged the drugged brewski? My knees shook as I stood. This was fucked. *I* was fucked.

When he turned on the taps to fill up the tub, the sound of rushing water echoed through the room. I took advantage of the noise to shake out my legs until the muscles began to respond. I was creeping toward the curtain separating the shower area from the bathroom when I heard an ominous *thud*. Then silence. Except for the gushing water pummeling the inside of the king-size tub.

Holy shit.

I didn't need to step out from behind the curtain to

see the body on the floor. I already knew what I'd find. He was supposed to drift off in a nice bath, not crash on the cold marble.

Head versus marble, never a fair fight.

As I stepped out from behind the curtain, hot steam assaulted my lungs. The floor was wet with it, and I lost my footing. I skidded, then fell. Conked my head.

That's how I lost my own battle with Queen Worth's bathroom marble.

Chapter Eleven

Ringo shook me by the shoulders and yelled in my face. The guy had gone totally mad. He held me too tight, occasionally slapping my face and repeating my name. *Vanna, Vanna*, he kept hollering in this anxious and annoying voice.

Who's the boss here, I tried to say, but my tongue wasn't cooperating. My lip hurt like hell. Fucking birds. Fucking jealous lovers. Fucking nights without sleep. What I needed was to lose consciousness again, so I did.

Black had become my color, and I basked in it like I was sunbathing on a moonless, starless night. Ah, nothingness, how I'd missed it. This drug induced coma was the best sleep I'd experienced in years. I waited for a dream to take me further out. I thought maybe I could dream myself out of my situation, out of my life, and wake up elsewhere.

No such luck. One minute, nothing, then a sudden *whoosh* and I was shocked into consciousness by a piercing onslaught of ice cold water.

I opened my eyes, and this time I was not alone. Ringo held me in his arms. Big, strong, and pissed off Ringo.

Wet Ringo.

He had me pinned up against one tile wall, and he was forcing me to stand under a laser spray of freezing water. Since all four shower heads were on, both of us were being doused by surround sound ice water. His clothes clung to his body and water sluiced off his head.

I wanted to laugh. A cold shower? Served him right for leaving me.

But wait. Maybe he hadn't left me.

"The hell you doing here?" I sputtered.

"Thank god. Thought you'd never snap out of it. Thought you were FTD."

I tried to stand on my own so he could shut off the damn water. My teeth were chattering, my head ached, and my lip was too painful to even think about.

"I leave you alone for a few days and look at you. You're a fucking mess, Van."

His teeth were chattering, too. I laughed, but it sounded more like a death gurgle.

Speaking of death gurgles. "Where's the bad husband?" I whispered.

Holding me up with one cold arm, he reached behind me to shut off the water. He propped me against the wall, and somehow I managed to remain upright.

The humidity of the room was a welcome relief. It was quiet, too. The bath was no longer running, and the music had stopped. I stood before my former assistant, shivering and pathetic and sickeningly happy.

I guess I was still drugged out because eventually it dawned on me. Ringo didn't seem happy. Not at all. In fact, the look he gave me sent chills down my spine. Or maybe that was from the ice water immersion. His white tee was plastered to his back, his cargo shorts soaked through. I could see his wallet through the cotton. I could see everything through the wet material.

Wait, maybe he *was* happy to see me.

"All over America," he said in a stern voice. "All over the fucken world. There are bad husbands populating every country on the damn planet. Not our responsibility. We can't kill 'em all." He shook his head, and water droplets splashed around us. "Enough's enough. We're officially retiring. I'm making an executive decision, here."

Like he could do that? Not even close.

I couldn't point that out to my assistant at that particular moment, however, since I was incapable of thinking clearly. The discussion would come later, along with the anger, blame, and hostile accusations.

As we emerged from the behind the striped curtain, me limping, Ringo supporting me, both of us iced through and slippery, I said, "Maybe we can revamp our business plan. Tweak it. Repurpose ourselves."

Then I saw the body on the floor. The *naked* body on the floor. One with a blood pool next to the head.

"What we need to do is, we need to tweak *this*. Make it look like an accident," Ringo said, speaking my more cluttery thoughts aloud. Until he had to go and add, "Better hope this one lives, Vanna. Because if he don't, we're dead in the water. Like he was supposed to be."

In other words, the gig was totally fucked. Due to my numerous mistakes. How had I been so careless, so stupid? After seven years of impeccable service to my clients, what had gone wrong with my business model? What had gone wrong with *me*? Was I incapable of functioning efficiently now unless I had a man on hand to assist me?

The thought chilled me more than the ice water bath had.

I edged closer to Tristan. He was still breathing, fortunately. He wasn't dead, just out. And he didn't look all that messed up, considering. But the situation was grim. Yes, indeed, I'd really fucked up this time. If I hadn't, bad hubby would've climbed into the tub, beer-filled glass in hand. Within minutes, he would have zoned out. I would've made sure his head dipped below the surface of the water and remained submerged. Nothing I hadn't done before.

Such a basic plan, a fool-proof method I've used several times with one hundred percent success. One of the easy-going no-lift methods I'd relied upon when I was on my own with my ex-terminations. Drug overdose is usually a sure bet if you do it right. Everyone accepts it as just another tragedy triggered by the careless combination of alcohol and pain meds. In this country, drug-related deaths exceed all other causes, including car accidents and shootings. So many people die from the misuse of prescription drugs nowadays, their deaths barely register. Unless the deceased is a celebrity.

Tristan was an unknown. My plan should've worked. But I'd screwed it up. The current situation could lend itself to an investigation. An unsolicited overdose, a suspicious bathroom incident involving the young husband of a super-wealthy cougar? The possibility of an attempted homicide on the estate belonging to a Palm Beach socialite? This might grab the interest of the press. And the police.

If everything had gone according to plan, the relieved widow would have been able to publically reveal her young husband's unfortunate narcotic addiction. To defray any possible suspicions, the grieving widow would be sure that her absence was corroborated, her emotional devastation made keen and obvious. And Dominique Viscoti Premini would have been yet another satisfied client offering the full cash payment for the special services provided by Ex-Treme Measures.

But no. Instead, due to my inexcusable incompetence, Ringo and I stood over a bad husband wacked out on Dilaudid, his handsome head bleeding from where he'd smacked it on the rim of the tub. Which had filled, then overflowed before Ringo got to it. We could move the guy into the tub now but, if he died, a medical investigator would determine that the head wound came first. They would be able to tell he had died on the floor, not in the tub. My plan had gone to shit.

I sighed. If he didn't die, our client would be mad as hell. She would not be replacing her retainer with cash. There would be no bonus. In fact, we'd be destroying her retainer check as soon as we got back to the office.

The office.

An electric jolt shot up through my weak calves, circulated around my chilled chest, and pulsed through my stitches. Mrs. Emworth. Was she still waiting for me at the office? Lying in wait would be a more accurate description.

Another angry woman. My life was full of them. Dangerous women, deceitful women, manipulative women. Mrs. Viscoti Premini had a right to be pissed at me. Mrs. Emworth was another story. I didn't know what her trip was, or why I was in it. Maybe she had a secret plan. Maybe she'd been hired to entrap me, hand me over to the authorities. Or maybe she wanted to ensnare me in her own devious plot to relieve me of the money I'd earned. From other angry women.

My mind flickered, and my legs shook. It was all too much. Too extreme. Ex-treme.

I bent forward, letting the blood pool in my head. I didn't want to be another body on the floor, so I held hard to my conscious state. This made my brain throb. And guess what? After about a minute, my lip hurt even more.

"Usually we don't *take* the knockout meds. We give them to the mark," Ringo said. "And who chewed your lip off?"

"Not now," I said. Only it sounded like *hot how*. Without lifting my head, I pointed to the problem husband. He lay on one side, as if curled up in sleep. His ass was bony, and all his ribs stuck out. He looked un-American, like he hadn't ever eaten at a fast food joint in his life. I felt like reviving him and feeding him porridge from a big bowl. Doughnuts and cream cheese. French fries. "What about him?" I asked Ringo.

"I checked his pulse when I came in. Normal. Better than yours." Ringo glared at me until I regained the upright position, which wasn't easy. "Lucky for us, he's got a hard skull. Not sure what's in there, but it seems to have stayed in there." He walked toward the vanity. "Let's grab the beer bottle and get out of here. Gimme the clean bottle, and I'll substitute it. We can leave him, let him try to figure it out when he comes to."

"What if he goes to the hospital, asks the doctors for tests to determine why he passed out like that?"

Ringo squinted at me, then chuckled. "You sound

like the African Greys, except you're even harder to understand. I think I know what you're gettin' at, though." He paused. "Think about it, Van. If he figures out he was drugged, he'll blame it on his wife. Who else? And maybe he'll be smart enough to roll the fuck outta here. I sure hope so, because when she comes home and finds him still hangin' around, all whiney with a bloody bandage on his head, she's gonna take a shit fit."

"It's a shit starter, all right," I agreed. "But he might bleed out if we leave him here."

Ringo shook his head. "He's fine. Small cut, a lump, nothing serious. Scalp injuries bleed a lot, making them look worse than they are. You know that. Although there's always the risk he's suffered a concussion."

As I handed him the clean and empty beer bottle, he gave me a strange look. I guess he wasn't used to being the brains of the operation. A thought which sobered me. Maybe *I* was the one with the head injury?

Ringo wrapped an arm around my shoulder and pulled me close. "Come on, let's get out of this depressing joint. Get you home, get us both cleaned up. This guy'll wake up soon enough, feel like a fool. Kinda like you must feel right about now."

Normally, I would've elbowed him or told him to shut his big mouth, but I was concentrating on walking across the room without collapsing. One foot in front of the other could mean the difference between leaving as fast as possible and embarrassing myself further. The back of my head pulsed in time with the lip. My pain was all synched up. The other good news...my sunburn didn't sting anymore. Maybe the cold shower had cured it.

Ringo left me leaning against the door jamb while he retrieved the St. Pauli Girl bottle from the vanity. As he jammed the cap back on, he gave me another accusatory look.

"Mark didn't even drink all of it. What'd you lace it with, horse tranqs from the vet's?"

In the past, I'd helped myself to a number of interesting tranquilizers while visiting my birds' doctor. The Dilaudid was from another source, however. Pain clinics were raking in the cash all over South Florida, and they were only too happy to prescribe you a prescription drug or two or three. I'd been advised to use the liquid hydromorphone hydrochloride for pain, and now I had. Mine, and someone else's.

I shrugged, tried to smile at Ringo. But my mouth hung open and a spinnaker of drool came out instead. Like I was fresh out of the dentist's office.

"Impressive," he said before hoisting me over one shoulder like a sack of cement.

I clung there, absorbing the damp heat from his broad back. He didn't seem to be hampered by the hundred and thirty pound dead weight. In fact, he made a cute little joke. "This is one position we haven't tried."

I was glad he spoke in the present tense. Maybe he hadn't left me in that way, either.

On our way through the master bedroom, I checked the digital alarm clock by the bed. Twenty after nine. Too late; I'd stood up Mrs. Emworth. When I got my act together, I would give her a call and apologize, set up another meeting with her. I needed to find out what she was up to.

Although it was obvious I really wasn't in any condition to drive, we had no choice. We couldn't leave either of our cars behind. And it would be unwise to make any noise while we made our escape. No sense having the neighbors report suspicious activities later, if it came to that. So, after he dumped me behind the wheel, Ringo told me to shift into neutral. He pushed the car from the rear, easing it down the driveway. With me steering in a half-assed manner, we rolled the Cabriolet south on A1A. The road was deserted, and fortunately, our trip was downhill.

We were quiet, and no cars passed by. Nearby, the silver speckled ocean eased itself onto the shore with a soft hiss. Up above, the stars cast light our way. They seemed too close, like giant floodlights.

Ringo stopped pushing, and my car slowed to a stop before a long dirt driveway. Off in the distance, a house sat hidden in the middle of a dark forest of slash pines, sea grape trees, and spikey palms. The estate belonged to Queen Worth's nearest neighbors.

"These asshats winter in Panama," Ringo whispered. He stood beside me in the starlight. "They think Florida's too cold."

Maybe because they lived in a sunless jungle.

Ringo pointed to the Escalade, parked in a thatch of cabbage palms. "Wait here and follow me home. Drive slow, Van." Like I was the assistant, and he was in charge.

He also insisted on taking the lead the entire way back to my place, crawling down A1A as if we were in a funeral procession. Going twenty-five miles an hour, just to make sure nothing happened to poor, fucked up Vanna.

Of course, I'm not a total bitch. I understood what was happening. I knew he was being a gentleman. Considerate, caring, patronizing. Once I reinstated my normal level of control over my mind and body, I planned to also reinstate my superior status in the relationship.

Ringo was, apparently, still my assistant. He needed to be reminded who was in charge.

Chapter Twelve

A hot shower helped to revive me. My assistant took a quick shower after I did, wrapping himself in one of the terry cloth robes from my rather large collection. All stolen from hotels I'd vacationed in with Ashton. I had on a purloined robe myself, a white shorty, thigh-length with a rope-cord tie.

When Ringo joined me, a bottle from my Guinness stash in hand, I was sitting out on the porch watching the birds sleep. They were huddled together on Popeye's perch. I had to admit, they were cute little fuckers.

"What's with that?" Ringo squeezed in beside me on the couch. His robe was ludicrously tight. He was nothing like my ex, not in any way. "That scary bitch took him on after all?"

I nodded. Silent communication would allow me to rest my battered lip. I shrugged, as if to say, *Who can predict the way love might manifest?* Then I reached for my cell and handed it to him.

"You want me to check the messages?"

I nodded a little too vigorously, which hurt. My stitches had loosened and the back of my head pounded, but I wasn't about to take something to ease the pain. I'd had enough pain medication to last me a good long while.

My assistant held my phone to his ear. He frowned,

staring over at me until I shifted around and lay down. I put my sore head in his lap and gazed out through the screening. An armada of soft white clouds streaked across the black sky. They marched quickly, with purpose, as if they had somewhere to be. I wanted to pull a pillow over my head and hide. I felt exactly how I looked, and I looked like shit. I didn't want anyone staring at my face, not tonight.

"Mrs. Emworth. Whoa. Bitching you out for not being at the office. What? She expected you to meet her there *tonight*? Wonder what she had planned, the tricky witch. Maybe she was all wired up." He clicked through a few more messages, half listening as he talked. "Here she is again, the entitled bitch. Wow. You know, I don't get her. I mean, I think they're workin' for somebody else, her and Jojo. I can't figure those two out. Are they a couple, partners maybe? Not sure, but I did a little snooping around while we were...not speaking these last few days. And—"

He stopped talking to listen to another message. Then he put it on speaker phone. I could feel his body tense up, the muscles tightening against mine. Poor Ringo did not deal well with competition.

"Hey, baby. Sorry to call so late. Oh, wait, it's not late. It gets dark so early these days. What month is it anyway? Look, I need to see you tomorrow. Please don't say no." Ashton made a weird sound, like a suffocated kiss. "Thanks, I really appreciate what you do for me. I know I've been difficult with the addictions and all, but I'm getting it under control and—"

"Oh, fuck me, I can't listen to this asshole anymore," Ringo muttered as he shut off the phone.

When he shifted his legs like he wanted me off them, I sat up again. He cleared his throat, as if he had a speech he needed to recite. Which he did. "Can't we leave all this bullshit behind? Go somewhere else, live a normal life? Think about it, Vanna. I can be a security guard. You could go back to school. Become a journalist. Write. Or raise birds. Hand-raise parrots. Whatever you want. Because this totally sucks. The clients are fucken nightmare horrible. We're not makin' the money we used to. And the emotional hold this drug-addicted loser has on you just blows my mind."

It was my turn to stiffen. Even though he was right. "I thought we might rebrand ourselves and stick around. What about that idea? I have debts to settle. We have clients to contend with. We can't just leave."

Every word I said sounded like *smush.*

Ringo cocked his head. "Huh? Whatever you said, I can tell it's a no." He looked out at the night sky. "Gotta say, you are absolutely the least *female* chick I've ever met. Ever! But I don't get you at all sometimes. Maybe I just don't understand the whole chick race."

Chick race?

I would've laughed, but I was afraid of ripping my stitches. I might've even admitted that I don't always get me either. But everything seemed too garbled to explain. It was useless trying to express myself. I leaned over and kissed him softly.

Then I screamed. My lip hurt like a mutha'.

****

The dream is the same, but there are endless variations. I am alone. I am lost. I am running. Often, there is a strange city in the distance, and I see the sharp angles of the buildings, the spires, bridges, and neon lights. Sometimes, I am running there, but I don't know why. Sometimes, I am already there, running through the streets, past the dark places, the black alleys and trash strewn corners that smell of urine and vomit and dead things. In the cleaner parts of town, I might stop to window shop, to gaze into busy cafes and restaurants. I look hungrily at the food, the drinks, the pretty people, lovers in tight huddles and lovely families with their arms around one another. I look at the glittering array of things I cannot have. I might stop to wonder why I am always running, why I am hurrying past the things that seem to make everyone else so content.

An old dream, I've had it many times. It always ends the same way.

Just before I woke up the morning after the fiasco at Mrs. Viscoti Premini's, I found myself in the dream again. I was running in a bright city full of well-heeled partiers, blazing shops, and bustling nightclubs. The streets were crowded, so crowded I was forced to slow to a walk. Then, suddenly, Ringo was walking beside me.

"It's because you reject the culture of emptiness," he said. But his lips didn't move when he spoke. He didn't even turn his head to look at me. He brushed past, and I heard him say, "You reject comfort because your brain is filled with sponge cake and your memories land there like a swarm of bees."

I tried to catch up to him, but he was lost in a swirl of young people dressed in tight bright clothing. They surrounded me too until they all surged into a doorway for a loud dark club. I looked around, but Ringo was gone.

Someone called my name. Brad Dickensen strolled up beside me, still oiled for the beach, still in his mankini. Handsome but dangerous looking, even if he was mostly naked. I looked away, embarrassed for him, but he seemed oblivious.

"Sew your shadow back on, Wendy," he told me with a sniper's snide smile. "And you might just save your own life."

What was with the Peter Pan reference? He stared at me, unblinking. The man had assassin eyes. I shrugged him off. I picked up speed, pushing past him, shoving my way through the clots of city dwellers and late-night revelers.

Dick didn't follow me, but I jogged onward. Then, as soon as I had the space to really take off, I sped up. I ran and ran and ran. Until I lifted off the ground like a box kite in a sea breeze.

And I flew away.

That's when I woke up. In my dreams, I never fly for more than a minute or two, and whenever I do, I awaken. This does not help me with my insomnia, but flying is the coolest feeling in the world. It's almost worth losing sleep over.

When I rolled out of bed, the sun had yet to rise. I felt strong again, solidly back in my body. My head felt okay. My lip was more mobile, and the swelling had gone down.

In the bathroom, I examined the stitches in the mirror over the sink, looking for signs of infection. I was surprised to see how clear my eyes looked. It does wonders for your appearance when you actually sleep, even if it's interrupted now and again by sudden cold showers or naked male bodies. I'd been traipsing around dreamland for more than the recommended eight hours, if you counted the knockout period in Mrs. Viscoti Premini's shower stall.

Using the bare finger method, I brushed at my teeth, gently, gingerly. Nothing bled, a wonderful sign. With a hand mirror, I was able to locate the bump on the back of my head that had been pounding nails in my skull when I collapsed into bed the night before. It was small, nothing to worry about. I patted my hair, pushing frizz-curls into place around the lump, creating the semblance of a hairdo. Which didn't look all that bad, considering the previous day's events.

I headed for the kitchen to make myself a strong cup of Colombian dark roast. Definitely not a running day, not with these head wounds. No, today's schedule had already been arranged for me. I would go straight to the office and prepare for the onslaught. Who would attack first? A furious Mrs. Emworth? The disappointed Queen Viscoti Premini? Maybe Mrs. Grady's lawyer would call or the always amusing Bella Cantor.

Before I reached the kitchen doorway, a huge dark figure rose from the living room couch. I screamed so loud I woke up the birds. Between outraged squawks, Porsche yelled, "Goldbrickin' ass."

"That's a new one," the intruder said. "She's got quite the vocab."

My heart beat a drum solo in my chest. Sinking into an arm chair, I said, "Ring, I'm going to kill you."

"I wouldn't be the first," he joked. He stood over me, naked except for a tight pair of jockey shorts. He seemed to be examining my face in the dim light cast by a streetlight out front. "Except for how all the color's drained from your face, you look a lot better."

I tried not to feel flattered. "The hell you doing here? I thought you went home after you finished your beer."

I'd been in too much pain the night before to do much but drop into bed and crash out. I'd left him on the porch with the birds and his Guinness.

"You never stay over," I added after an uncomfortable silence.

"Wonder who won't let me," he said. "Oh, yeah, I remember. The same woman who offs rich slobs for their angry wives and uses the money to pay for her sick-fuck husband's drug problem. Oh, yeah, now I remember." He slapped his forehead, rolled his eyes.

"Whoa. What's with you today?" No nookie makes big boy cranky. I stood and headed for the kitchen. "Is my devoted assistant a widdle bit gwumpy before he has his morning coffee?"

He followed me in, and we both blinked hard when I snapped on the track lights. I fetched the coffee from the freezer and got right to work on the morning brew. I was all about forgiving and forgetting.

But Ringo wasn't. "Can we have the rest of that talk now? The one we started after you did drugs on the job and I had to rescue you from the client's bathroom?"

I poured bottled water into my decade old coffee maker and counted out the scoops of ground beans, dumping them into the filter. The aroma was delightful. I was starved and thirsty. I really didn't want to have this conversation. Not now, not ever.

But Ringo wouldn't let it go. He stood next to me, talking. "I gotta rebook the flights. We're in the system. We got the air miles. I just need to reschedule us. So let's decide where and I'll book us and we can just go. Today, tonight, tomorrow first thing. I don't wanna deal with the fallout from the Viscoti Premini disaster, and I'm worried about the rest of them clients. They're all turnin' on us, Van. It's like a fucken zombie movie. Night of the Rich Dead."

I switched on Mr. Coffee, wondering how well I would be able to swallow. Could I handle an English muffin? Wait, was he still talking?

"We had a good thing. Now it's not so good. So hey, it's time to roll. Admit it, Van. We're done here." He followed me to the freezer like a hungry puppy.

The English muffins were frozen so I popped them in the microwave to thaw them out. In one cupboard, I found an old jar of orange marmalade and a box of Cheerios, and in the fridge I unearthed a quart container of pineapple juice. I rinsed out two dusty souvenir mugs from the Hemingway House in Key West, arranged everything on the table, and returned to the coffee machine to wait for the pot to fill.

Ringo stood by the refrigerator watching me, his arms crossed on his big bare chest. "Are you giving me the silent treatment? Or does your lip still hurt too much to talk?"

As I poured the coffee, I nodded toward one of the stools at the kitchen island. Ringo sat down. Good boy, at least he was taking some of my orders again. I returned my attention to the muffins. They'd need to be toasted next.

With my back to my assistant, I said, "I'm not going anywhere, Ring. I can't. I can't just run away because the clients are entitled assholes and they act strange, deranged, or threatening. This is nothing new.

It's part of the work we've chosen. Except for last night's fuck-up, which was a freak show and, I admit, all my fault. Which is part of why I have to hang in there and make things right again."

"You said last night you wanted to tweak the business, recreate the model. That's fine with me. As long as we can stop trackin' down dirty dogs and do some other kind of investigative work. And as long as we do it in some other town, some distant part of the world. Because we can't stay here, Van. If we do, one of these jokers is gonna drive up in a limo and bite us in the ass."

The toaster oven dinged, and I slid the browned muffin halves onto paper plates. I wasn't much for domestic duties. I was all about efficiency and avoiding chores. Like washing dishes or shopping for dishware after the ex absconded with all the wedding china. Or was that just an excuse? Was I still waiting for him to come home, bringing his grandmother's silver tea set with him? Why would I be so irrational? He'd probably traded everything worth anything for a plug of something nasty.

Ringo must have read my mind or picked up a marital vibe floating around the kitchen or something. He stood up, letting the stool tip over behind him. "It's that prick, isn't it? You won't leave with me, even to save your own hide from a legal battle. The threat of jail's not even enough. Because you're still stuck on rescuing that brain-dead husband of yours. Right? I know I'm right. I know you."

He knew me, all right. But I wasn't about to cop to that. "Sit down, please, and eat with me. Let's not go at one another right now. We need to keep chill and get through the shit storm together. We can fix everything. I know we can. If we stay calm."

I set the plates down and started to dump marmalade on the muffins. He grabbed my wrist and held it there while globs of gooey jam dripped off the dollar store butter knife in my hand. I looked him in the eye.

His face was fierce. "No, we can't. Did you hear me, Vanna? I said *no*."

He let go of me, but I didn't dare move, not even to reach for my coffee. Which I needed. And some food, because what I really needed right then was sustenance. Not a lecture from my assistant. My cute but not exactly brilliant assistant.

"I wanted to leave days ago, Van, and you refused. Now our situation's worse. We have no clients waiting to pay us, only clients who either want to screw us or get their money back. Possibly both. This is the new economics, in case you haven't noticed—screw or be screwed. Right now looks like our turn to bend over. Well, I ain't doin' it. I'd rather navigate *now*. While I still have that option."

I was losing him again. He'd switched to the singular. No more plural. No more *us* and *we*. So I reached for my coffee. Because there was nothing else I could do. I saw exactly where this discussion was headed.

Men pick fights as an excuse to leave. I remind my clients of this tactic on a regular basis. Better not to participate. I sipped the coffee, and oh, it was excellent.

My stomach growled. When had I last eaten? I plopped myself down on a stool and ripped off a chunk of one of the muffin halves, dunking it in my coffee.

Then I eased it past my lip and into my mouth, letting it fall apart on my tongue. I chewed thoroughly, swallowed carefully.

If my assistant hadn't been hovering over me, giving me the evil eye, I would've grinned. I could eat! Soon enough, I would heal up. Then maybe I'd look like a human being again.

"I'm tired of getting other people's shit on my shoes, Van. I'm outta here. Unless you got somethin' to say?"

I had nothing to say so I said exactly that.

He stomped out of the room. He didn't stop to pick up the stool he'd knocked over, either. I dunked and swallowed the rest of my muffin, then scraped off the excess marmalade I'd spread on the muffin half intended for my assistant. I dunked his share in my coffee and ate it. Next up, cereal.

While I was in search of a clean plastic bowl, Ringo popped his head in the room. He was dressed in his tee and shorts from the day before. "I'm outta here."

I found a bowl without any cracks in it and filled it with the breakfast of champions.

My assistant was still talking. "I'll need the back pay you owe me. I don't expect the usual cash bonus, since you fucked us out of it. I'll drop by on my way out of town. Soon. You better have my cash ready, Vanna."

He ducked when I threw the bowl, and it landed on the living room floor with a splurt and a loud crack.

After he left, I grabbed up the Cheerios box and ate a handful of dry cereal, which hurt. But only a little. I finished my coffee and poured myself a second cup before I cleaned up the mess we'd made.

Chapter Thirteen

The morning sun had yet to light up the sky, and the air was cold and dry. The dip in humidity felt like a special treat. I stood in the doorway and took a few deep breaths. Change was in the air. My life would be easier without a lover. I'd feel less responsible, less burdened by someone else's expectations. And I could always hire a new assistant.

Or so I told myself.

Before leaving for work, I filled the birds' water cups and set out some fruit, trying not to envy them for their sudden and somewhat nauseating devotion to one another. They preened each other and ignored me, as if I'd morphed from nurturer to wait-staff. I'd become an unwanted intrusion in their ongoing orgy of mutual admiration.

Gag me. Nothing like the end of an affair to make others' acts of affection seem revolting.

As I drove to the office, I tried to convince myself the changes I was facing were all for the best. It had been unprofessional to sleep with my assistant, and look where my bad behavior had landed me. *Sans* assistant. I would learn from this and be more careful about whoever I hired in the future.

Or so I told myself.

By the time I pulled into a space in front of Starbucks, however, I felt like shit. I could try to convince myself everything was fine. I could run that tape loop over and over, but I'd have a difficult time believing it. I knew myself too well. My heart pulsed a sad little song with a familiar refrain singing through the rest of my body. My gut ached with a specific stab, the kind I'd identified years ago as old grief. The grief that comes with abandonment. I felt queasy, too, jittery with the anxiety of knowing I was alone in the world.

All alone. Again.

My sad song. Ugh, even thinking about it made me sick at heart. And bored. I bored myself silly. I didn't want to have the kind of pathetic past I'd been saddled with. But who does?

My mother gave birth to me when she was only seventeen. My childhood was a cliché. The unwanted offspring of a girl too Catholic to abort me, too immature to raise me. But she tried her best, and for that I'll always be grateful. She had a lot of guts, my mom, and a gigantic heart. But she'd been dealt a bad hand and men were to blame. Always the losing hand, over and over, bad men her downfall every time.

My father was a South Boston Irish kid a few years older than my mom and totally uninterested in being a parent. He bartended at a neighborhood dump a few blocks from where we lived. He'd drop by every week or so, give my mother a little money, hold me in his thick arms. I remember the way he kissed me, a big wet smooch on the top of my head. I don't know if my mother loved him. She never said. All she did say was that he was a womanizer and he'd been rough on her. She didn't want him coming around me any more than he did.

Back in the late seventies, early eighties, the blue

collar men my mom brought home to our duplex apartment on L Street all seemed the same to me. They were interchangeable. Maybe my memory has blurred over time, but all I can recall are lanky losers with long, greasy hair and scruffy clothes. Men who smelled of smoke and whiskey. I didn't understand what my mother saw in them because she always ended up crying whenever one stayed over. And whenever one was around too much, my father stopped dropping by. I missed his silent hugs, his big warm presence.

When I was four years old, my mother married Seamus O'Hara. He wasn't any different than her previous boyfriends, equally rough around the edges, a heavy drinker. But Seamus stuck around longer.

My mother worked as a cashier at a family-owned convenience food market up the street from our apartment. The owners were kind to her. They let her bring me to work until I was old enough for preschool. I'd slept in a secondhand carriage, then a stroller, tucked behind the cash register. For years after that, I could hear the jingle of quarters and smell the papery odor of dollar bills in my sleep.

We got discounts on food, so that helped.

Not having the money for the things we needed was the focus of my home life. Money was my mother's obsession. My stepfather worked in construction, which meant he was often between jobs. Whenever he was earning, he was generous to us, I'll give him that. My mother put up with his irresponsible ways because she needed him to help support us. She allowed Seamus to walk all over her because she believed she'd be unable to pay the bills on her own.

But my mother and I were not the only females he

shared his paycheck with. And whenever he wasn't working, he disappeared. If he was hanging around, they fought. He turned surly, mean. I knew enough to keep my distance when Seamus had been out of work more than a few days in a row.

Even as a child of five or six, I was aware that my mother was a victim of her own ignorance and her dependence on men. Maybe love itself is a form of PI. Maybe love is simply that. Permanent Insanity. It seemed like that to me when I watched my mother cry herself to sleep.

I was determined to lead a different life than my mother's. No drag-me-down men, no feather destructive behavior. I pictured my future self as an independent woman. I made big plans for myself, plans that did not involve unreliable assholes. I would be self-made, self-employed. I'd earn my own way. No man would have to pay *my* bills.

My mom was big on education, she wanted me to have what she'd missed—a high school diploma and a college degree. To please her, I studied hard and did well in school. When I was eleven, I earned a scholarship to the prestigious Boston Latin. I loved that school. I had friends. I was on the girls track team. I excelled in declamation, made dean's list every semester.

My mother was so proud of me. She told me I'd be the first woman to make it up on The Wall, joining all the famous men who'd attended the school over its long history. My mother made sure I had the money I needed for my school uniform and a good pair of running shoes, a little spending money for makeup and an occasional outfit, a sweater, a pair of jeans. By the time

I was in ninth grade, she'd scored a receptionist job at a busy real estate office in Dorchester where she worked long hours and many weekends.

Back when I was in high school, my mother was younger than I am now. But she looked so old to me. She was terribly worn out. She subsisted on cigarettes and black coffee, and her insomnia kept her up many nights. As did the endless arguments with Seamus. I stayed at school as long as I could every day, studying in the library or running extra miles at the track. I hated to hear the things he said to her. It made me sick. It made me want him dead.

Then, when I was sixteen, he left. My mother fell into a depression so debilitating she stayed in bed for days at a time. She lost her job. She lost weight. She lost interest in life. In me. She drifted out of my life. The week before I turned seventeen, she died. An overdose of sleeping pills, washed down with a quart of cheap vodka. Maybe it was a mistake in judgment, but I doubt it. My mother didn't drink, not like that. Except on her last night on this dusty earth.

She'd always kept a rainy day fund and had somehow managed to leave behind a meager savings account. She also had a small life insurance plan. I knew I could eke out an existence from what she'd left me as long as I landed a job. But I had a problem. In the eyes of the state, I was too young to live alone. Also, my mother's tiny estate belonged to her absent husband. Legally, he was the heir.

The man could smell a penny in a sinkhole. Seamus rapidly reappeared, grief-stricken and apologetic. At the funeral, a bleak affair held at a Catholic church downtown, Seamus offered to come home. He said he would stay with me in our apartment on L Street until I turned eighteen.

The idea sickened me. I blamed him for my mother's depression, for her death. But there didn't appear to be a better option. There was no way I could deal with foster care, but without adult supervision, I would be forced by state law to move to a stranger's home. This was unacceptable to me. Horrifying, in fact.

I'd appealed to my biological father, but he'd recently married a girl a few years older than I was and there was no room for me in that arrangement. My mother's parents had written us off when I was born out of wedlock, and I would never forgive them for that. They'd shown no interest in me anyway. So, even though I blamed him for my mother's suicide, it turned out I needed my stepfather.

This infuriated me.

I was young, but I was not naïve. He didn't come near me, nothing that sordid. But he did burn through my mother's savings with his bar hopping, incessant partying, and generous hosting of a long line of fellow drunks. He brought home a lot of sad women. I kept my distance and became even more determined to make something of my life—without men in it.

To put food on the table, I got an afterschool job at the same market where my mother had worked all those years. I stood before the cash register where I'd slept as a baby, safe in my mother's care. Everyone was kind to me. At work, at school, in my neighborhood. But my heart hurt, and I had a stabbing pain in my gut. There was nothing physically wrong with me. I was alone, that was all.

Seamus's presence in my life was a necessary evil.

A maddening convenience. And, I began to realize, a strange opportunity. Waking up to the sound of him retching in the bathroom or giggling with some cheap girl from the bar, I realized how much power I could have. On my own. If I was willing to do what it took. If I chose to be the one making the decisions in my life.

I was only seventeen, the same age my mother had been when she'd first been fucked over by a man. This would not be my fate. Women did not have to be powerless. And men didn't deserve to be happy at everyone else's expense.

Within a year, Seamus O'Hara was dead.

****

When I came out of Starbucks with a double caramel latte, I almost tripped over him. He'd been waiting for me out front like an unkempt, unwanted mutt.

"I'm not stopping at the bank today," I informed Ashton.

I wasn't in the mood for my not-ex. His continued presence in my life had contributed to the blowup with Ringo, and I was starting to hate myself for not being more proactive. Really, why wasn't the guy an ex, already?

The thought of dumping him in the Atlantic brightened my mood for a second, lighting up my heart with a tiny flare of optimism. This bright spot in my day was fleeting. Of course I couldn't dispose of my husband. Not if I wanted a cut of his family wealth. Not if I wanted to stay in business. Not if I wanted to keep my nose clean in this town.

I kept walking. "I never agreed to a meeting, Ash. I'm busy."

He gave me one of those zombie stares. When I looked in his reddened eyes, I could barely see my former husband in there. Not in his gaunt face, not in the baggy clothes, the haggard, unwashed frame. It was as if my husband had been kidnapped by aliens, sucked out of his body and replaced with a bad imitation. I shivered, tried to brush past him and escape to my car.

"We need to talk." His hand on my wrist was ice cold. Now I'd have to sanitize my arm. I pulled away, but he hung on, wheedling, "Please, Vanna. Please just sit for a minute. I promise I'll make this real quick."

"Now? Here?"

I looked around. The cool weather and early hour had created an unusual situation. We had the tables in front of Starbucks all to ourselves. I sighed, pulled up a black metal chair, and perched on the edge. "Okay, what do you want this time?"

He sat across from me, reeking of cigarette smoke and something else. Something worse. Day-old bacon grease?

"Your face looks bad," he said. "Did the big ape slap you around?"

I choked out a dry laugh. "No, of course not. You know nobody pushes me around." I wondered if he even remembered how many times he'd been pecked, and pecked hard, by my African Grey. "Popeye has a new girlfriend, and she's the jealous type."

It was his turn to laugh. "Wow, so your love slave finally made it with someone else. Never thought that featherbrained momma's boy had it in him. Good for him."

He was altogether too cheerful about my injury and its cause. I scowled, which stretched at my stitches.

"One minute, then I split. Some of us still work for a living."

"That's what I need to talk to you about. Your work."

He looked over his shoulder, carefully checking the quiet street behind him before turning to face me again. Ashton's been paranoid for years. What drug addict isn't?

I didn't pay much attention to his behavior. Instead, I set the timer on my phone and placed it between us on the table. "Fifty seconds."

"The cops are on to you, Vanna. They know what you and your simian friend are up to. They came to me with a deal. Don't worry, I turned it down. But I'm here to warn you, these guys aren't fucking around. Methinks you're in big doo-doo this time. You're on the edge of losing it all."

He was lying, of course. What drug addict doesn't? He would never turn down a deal. Nor would he offer to help me, not unless there was something in it for him. Like earning some kind of payoff.

Possibilities raced through my mind. Maybe Ashton had found out about the special services offered by Ex-Treme Measures and was going to blackmail me. Or else he'd been picked up for drug possession and was using me as a lure in order to avoid going to jail. Maybe the cops suspected me of something and my not-soon-enough-ex was wired.

Could there be a transmitter under that unzipped jacket? I looked at my near-ex's narrow chest. Was that a lump beneath the dirty plaid of his wool shirt?

Now *I* was acting paranoid.

"I have no idea what you're talking about," I said

with a straight face. Cold sweat dripped between my breasts. "I run a reputable investigative agency, and we do not break any laws. If you think you can slander me and my company to escape what is probably proper punishment for your own crimes, you are dead wrong."

I emphasized the *dead.* Just to see his face, which showed nothing. The guy was an empty suit, but without the suit. He was an empty pile of old clothes. Smelly old clothes. He had pigeon feathers in his hair, for god's sake.

My cell beeped, and I stood up, sliding the phone back in my leather satchel. I fluffed my own feathers, getting ready to fly.

"They know what you've done, Vanna. These guys are detectives. They've been on your case for over a year. They told me they have a list of names. What're you two doing? Threatening stupid Palm Beachers with dirty photos?"

If he didn't know, I wasn't about to tell him. "Time's up, dipshit. You've insulted me and my assistant. I'd be upset, but why bother? Your brain is pickled. You don't even know what you're saying. I think you're making this whole thing up just to get more money out of me. So here's my response, for the record. *Fuck* you."

I leaned in, face to face with what was left of the love of my life. "And from now on, you're to leave me alone. I want you a hundred feet away from me and my assistant. No more contact, no calls, no visits. Or, believe me, I'll get a restraining order. Then I'll be the one making a deal with the cops."

I stomped off, leaving the latte on the table. Which was stupid, I wanted my coffee. I stomped back to the table.

As I snatched up the cardboard cup, my ex looked at me with a mournful expression. "If you go down, I go down, V." His nickname for me, back when we were in love. A hundred years ago. It made me cringe just to hear him say it. "I'll die without you."

"I can't save you, Ash. I never could. From now on, you're on your own. I'm out. I should've backed off a long time ago. You don't need me. You just think you do. You won't die without my handouts. And maybe, just maybe, you'll do what it takes to save yourself."

He hunched over the small table, looking like the beaten dog he'd become. My long-held feelings for him evaporated, replaced with a kind of cold calm.

Why had I hung on to the hope of reconciliation with this man? With any man? I'd learned the difficult truth early on. They're all the same. Interchangeable. Nothing but heartache and pain.

Back when I fell for him, I thought Ashton Treme was different. Not like Seamus, not like my dad, not like my mother's other men. Ash was not a loser back then. He was charming. He'd led a charmed life. A dreamy childhood in the soft light of upper class wealth. All the best schools, tutors, and coaches. Glamorous ski trips and snorkeling lessons, vacations in the islands. Summers with his parents' people on the French Riviera. All you can pick designer clothes and fancy sports cars. The six-figure C-suite position at daddy's company. Ash had been sweet, bright, and fun. He had money. And he loved me.

Or so I thought. Until he threw it all away for some scuzzy young druggie and a harsh life on the street. How could he throw *me* away like that?

As I walked briskly to my car, I could hear Dr. Trainor's voice in my head. *Pair bonds too often become pair bondage.*

When I pulled away from the curb, I felt something brittle snap inside me. My heart warmed, and I was flooded with relief. A small but essential part of me soared up and away.

The sense of freedom that followed was better than a Dilaudid high. Much better.

****

Mrs. Cantor was waiting for me in the hall outside my office door. Where was Ringo when I needed him? Oh, yeah, packing for a one-way flight to the other side of the world.

"I need to talk to you," she told me. "I got ten minutes, then I'm late for work."

Like it was my fault she hadn't called to schedule an appointment. I unlocked the door and stepped back, allowing her to enter first. "I don't usually see clients before nine, but—"

"You don't have any clients with my problems, though, do you? I could go to prison for this, and I don't know what to do. I already paid the hitman—"

I stopped her right there, hustling her inside, and slamming the door behind us. "Mrs. Cantor, I do not want to hear about any illegal activity you may have undertaken. But I do have some good news for you. Your husband is fine. From what I could determine, Mr. Cantor is unharmed. He's hiding out, spending time away. Away from *you.* Staying safe under his lawyers' supervision. This means—"

"This means I'm still in trouble. He knows I tried to—"

"Mrs. Cantor. Please listen." I wanted to strangle the woman. Why was she still talking? I held up a hand to stop her, speaking loudly enough to drown out her annoying Brooklyn accent. "Your husband's fine. All he wants is for you to leave him alone. He wants to live his life without you in it. Can you agree to his request? If you can, I doubt he'll accuse you of anything."

She sank onto the couch with a sigh, and I sat down across from her.

"You'll need to agree to an uncontested divorce. He'll take his stuff, you'll take yours, and your partnership will end. Just like with any other business arrangement. Simple. Okay?"

When she opened her mouth, I held up the hand again. "Yes or no, Mrs. Cantor. Yes?"

She nodded. Her chins waggled, and her droopy hair fell forward, wisping across her pale face.

I glanced at the clock over her head. "It's almost nine. You should go."

She stood up, rearranging her bulky skirt over her wide hips. I wanted to say something supportive, but I couldn't think of anything. *Get yourself some psychological help*, was all that came to mind.

"Thank you, Ms. Treme," she said in the softest voice I'd ever heard her use. "I want you to know how grateful I am for your help." She stepped forward and hugged me. "I still love him, but I also hate him," she whispered. "I guess I'm willing to let him go."

I patted her shoulder. "Good choice."

After closing the door behind her, I let out a prolonged sigh. I felt sorry for the lady, but she was a fool. A dangerous fool. Her violent anger at being dumped by her husband might have ruined her life. And my business.

In our culture, middle-aged women don't have it easy. They often end up on the shit end of the stick, used up and tossed out. Maybe this is caused by innate animal behavior, maybe it's due to a youth-obsessed population with short attention spans. Whatever the cause, I'd capitalized on it. And I'd been sure my business model would hold up. The market seemed so vast. So many angry, betrayed, about to be dumped wives, just waiting to pay for my special services.

Lately, however, the erratic behavior of my clientele was making it difficult for me to help women in need. Ringo's attitude hadn't helped, nor had my own screwups. Besides, why was I even bothering to wage a one woman crusade against the vast population of bad men? Why not let nature take its course?

When my phone rang, I checked the caller ID. Mrs. Viscoti Premini. Out of her mind, probably, with disappointment and concern. What went wrong? Why was her nitwit husband still a problem? What was the plan now? What would we do next?

I had no idea.

With that in mind, I let the call go to voice mail, joining the six unheard messages bearing Mrs. Emworth's ID.

I got out the shredder and went to work. Mrs. Viscoti Premini's retainer check went first, instantly reduced to skinny strips of worthless paper. Then Mrs. Emworth's hefty deposit. If I could've fit my head in the shredder, I might've taken care of my biggest problem right then and there.

If life was just a rough draft, I wanted to shred mine and start over.

Chapter Fourteen

Carrying a cardboard box filled with shredded paperwork, I locked my office door. Then I walked carefully down the stairs. My shoes squeaked across the heavily waxed floor. The lobby echoed its emptiness, as always. As I pushed the box and myself through the front door, a young man in bike shorts hurried past me into the building.

I let him go. Because I wasn't paying attention.

Eight or nine men clustered out in the street. They stood around my car.

One of them yelled, "Here she is."

My heart missed at least one beat. Then I recognized the bum attire of the homeless men from the lot across the street.

"Whaddup, guys?" I asked as I approached.

It was unusual to see them out on the street. They didn't want to get in trouble with the neighbors, so they avoided hanging around our cars, panhandling, or asking about odd jobs. Instead, they kept to themselves in the lot, where they maintained a low profile.

"What's the problem?" I set the box down next to my car.

"You got the problem, lady."

I recognized the guy with the waist-length dreadlocks. He stepped forward, blocking my path. Although he was relatively young, probably not much older than me, his face had aged, darkened from years of unscrubbed dirt and too much sun. Only his pale blue eyes were bright, youthful.

"Two hosers. They tried to break into your little junker here. But we spotted 'em, chased 'em off."

I felt like laughing. I'd been driving my old VW around the county for years and nobody had ever seemed interested before. I only bothered to lock it to protect the Boss CD player I'd installed. These cars were notoriously unreliable and mine was a rusty mess. Who would want the old thing?

Which is exactly what I asked the group in front of me. They stood quietly together, looking at me. "Who'd even want it?"

They exchanged glances, shifting uneasily. I smelled marijuana, sterno, and cheap beer.

Dreadlocks spoke up. "They weren't stealin' it. They were searchin' it."

My heart sank and something splashed around in my belly. Coffee mixed with apprehension, an unpleasant acidic combination. So Ashton had been telling the truth?

"Cops? They come in a black and white? Or a government issue sedan?"

Somebody laughed.

"We don't run cops off, lady. Not our style. These boys drove a Mercedes E550. New, black, big tint. Didn't catch the plate." Dreadlocks looked down at his sneakers. The laces were missing. "Both of 'em were built, pumped up, but not so tough. Else they wouldn't 've run off when we yelled at 'em."

He looked up again. When his eyes caught mine, he grinned. I sucked in a quick breath. Give this guy access to a shower and some astringent soap, and he could clean up real nice. He still had all his teeth. Automatically, I brushed my hair out of my face, straightened my shoulders, and returned his smile. What the hell was I doing? I'd finally left Ashton in my past, where he belonged, and now I was flirting with some other derelict?

I stopped leering at the homeless man before me and turned away. I needed to thank the group of milling men. My local bums. My heroes. "You guys are the best. Can I buy lunch?"

I fished in my bag for my wallet, pulling out a couple of twenties. I passed them to Dreadlocks before I slid the box into the back seat and climbed into my car. The boys muttered their thanks.

"Hey, you want to do me a favor and keep an eye on the building?" I called out as they wandered away. "Maybe you guys want some unofficial employment in the security business?"

They were already hurrying off. Forty bucks would buy a delirious amount of screw-top wine and quart beer.

But Dreadlocks strolled back, watching me. He stood by the driver's side window. "I'm listening."

"Nothing too taxing," I explained. "If these men return, see if you can get me a license plate number. You have a phone?"

He gave me a scathing look and pulled a new iPhone out of one of the front pockets of his filthy jeans. Even street people were carrying these days, thanks to our fine welfare system. Cell phones for emergencies, but not enough food to live on. And nothing to make a man, or woman for that matter, feel like a viable participant in the economic machine.

I handed him my business card. "Call me immediately if they show up. You see them again, I'll pay you for any details you can provide."

He nodded, backing off so I could pull out. When I looked in the rearview, he was still standing in the street, watching me drive away.

I ran the possibilities through my mind. The two guys interested in the contents of my car might be from Robes, Pierre, searching for more evidence against Mrs. Cantor. Or they might be working for Mrs. Grady, law types or thugs she'd hired to harass me. There was always Mrs. Viscoti Premini, who had every right to turn on me now that I'd failed to eliminate her most pressing financial problem.

The possibilities were many when I thought about it. What if they'd been sent by someone from my past or someone who'd been investigating one of my special services cases? The two beefy guys could be anyone, considering my long and seriously checkered personal and professional history.

On the way to my place, where I planned to burn my shredded paperwork in a steel canister I kept out back for such purposes, I did some serious life reviewing. I'd done well, considering my rocky start in life. I wasn't living in a parking lot, smoking weed and drinking Two Buck Chuck. I owned my own home, and I'd established a successful small business. I had money in the bank, a decent wardrobe, and a semi-reliable vehicle. My abs were tight, I weighed what I had in high school, and my limbs were smooth and supple. Shit, I could still run five miles without feeling it the next day. My hair was thick, my teeth were strong, and my brain hadn't shorted out on me. Yet.

All of this was commendable. But when I was being ruthlessly honest with myself, I wasn't pleased with my life in all aspects. There was the matter of my relationships with the opposite sex. My men were all catch and release. At least twenty short-term lovers— but really, who kept count?—one useless husband, and more than a dozen dead male bodies littered my past. And now I was getting all wet and gooey for the homeless bum who lived in the empty lot across from my office? Maybe my brain *was* starting to misfire.

The Cabriolet labored toward downtown, stalling out at each successive traffic light. My car needed a tune-up. So did I. As much as I hated to admit it, I needed an adjustment in my life, notably with my attitude toward men.

Of course, it all started with my childhood. A shrink would have a lot to work with. But that was never going to happen. I wasn't Tony Soprano, I couldn't talk to a professional. I would have to work it all out for myself.

When I thought about it, I could see where my attitude had gone off track. If that's what you wanted to call it. My stepfather had died of unknown causes. Unknown to everyone except me.

At the time, the coroner determined Seamus had hit his head on the windshield while his truck tumbled down a steep embankment off an icy back road north of Boston. He'd been speeding. He wasn't wearing a seatbelt. And his blood alcohol level was more than double the legal limit. The case seemed clear cut, another late-night drunk making stupid, ultimately fatal choices. Fortunately, nobody else had been hurt or, god forbid, killed.

The neighbors were happy to rat on the late Seamus O'Hara, describing him to investigators as a no-good drunk, a mooch who'd lived off his hard-working wife, then his hard-working stepdaughter. So there was never any question of guilt. Nobody suspected I was involved in my stepfather's accidental death.

Coincidentally, I'd turned eighteen the day of Seamus's demise. I was legally an adult, the rightful heir to what was left of my mother's small estate. Most of the money had been wasted on bar whiskey and loose women, but the remainder would help me get a start on my own life. Combined with my savings from my job at the store, I had what I needed to take off in search of myself.

So first thing I did after the funeral was purchase a one-way Amtrak ticket to Miami. And I had enough left over for me to begin a new, fully independent life.

That kind of success can go to your head. It definitely went to mine.

Don't get me wrong, it's not like I set out to become the kind of woman who knocked off unsavory men. I was not into vigilantism. I didn't ride into town on a white horse. But once I had the knowhow and found I had a lack of guilt after a justified hit, I moved in that direction. Shit happens.

My first lover in Miami was next on the hit list. A handsome hunk of a guy but an insane drunk, he had no idea who he was dealing with. One time he showed up with a bad attitude when I wasn't in the mood for it. It was late, and he was full of tequila, so I asked him to leave. He pushed his way inside my apartment, raped and beat me. I say one time, because it never happened again. In fact, not long after that, the guy disappeared. Poof.

I moved north to West Palm Beach, leaving any remorse I might have felt behind me.

After that, I became more careful with my affections. Took me long enough, right? Obviously, I hadn't yet figured out how not to be my mother. I was determined, however, not to repeat her mistakes. So I limited my affairs to brief sexual relationships with emotionally unavailable men while I took classes in martial arts and self-defense. In order to support myself, I worked multiple jobs—housekeeping for a wealthy retired couple, cleaning rooms at a luxury hotel on the beach, helping out with office work in the condo development where I lived. On weekends, I waitressed at a biker bar out in the Everglades.

The other weekend waitress was a warm, busty blonde from rural Alabama. When she came to work one Saturday with a black eye and a swollen jaw, I made her tell me what had happened. Her answer was predictable, but it really upset me. Her bad husband had wailed on her numerous times, and she hated him. But whenever she tried to leave him, he threatened to kill their three year old daughter.

I suggested she poison her husband with antifreeze. Her face was unreadable, but she nodded a little and smiled. Then she wandered off. I had been too blunt, and I regretted it. But when she came to me later that night for specific guidance, I told her I would be happy to provide an assist.

A few months later, I sat in the back row at his funeral. The church wasn't crowded, and my friend looked radiant in a short black dress. Nobody wept as the casket moved up the aisle. In fact, there wasn't a damp eye in the place.

At work the following weekend, she handed me an envelope stuffed with cash. "You saved my life. It's the least I can do."

That's when I first came up with the idea for Ex-Treme Measures. Surely, barmaids in biker joints weren't the only ones willing to pay me to save them from bad husbands. What about all the wealthy women who'd been hurt by their lousy spouses? Might they not be willing to shell out some serious money to make sure the problem was permanently solved?

Yes, the work was risky. But so often the law is not helpful to women in dire straits. Too often women in rocky relationships get hurt. Even killed. So do their children. And if they successfully defend themselves, they can go to jail. The law doesn't always do the right thing for victims of domestic violence. There are just too many casualties in the war between the sexes, and it seemed to me at the time that men were winning. Fists down.

What about restraining orders? Not worth the paper they're printed on. Show a bunch of legalese to a man with his wife's throat in his hands, and he'll spit in your face. And continue choking her. Shelters are full to the brim with women and kids trying to stay safe from out of control men. It's a sickening fact.

Then there are the cheats, the emotional abusers, the moochers and deviants. The ones who refuse to agree to a divorce, preferring to make their woman's life a living hell. What's a good wife to do? Not much she *can* do.

I figured if the law couldn't protect women from bad husbands, why not do the world a favor and get rid of the source of the problem? I tried to come up with a business model that could support my philosophy. Pitching my services to the rich women who needed them and offering free or discount assistance to those who could not afford to pay for help seemed like the best business plan to adopt. But how would I advertise? Market myself? Brand my business?

Then I met Ashton Treme. He was rich. I didn't need to work. I thought I'd made a good choice for myself, for my life. I forgot all about my crazy business idea.

Ashton was gorgeous back then. A handsome and clean looking man. He'd dropped by the lobby bar at the hotel where I was working as a chambermaid. It was happy hour, and I had scrubbed enough toilets to last me a lifetime. I strolled into the bar for a can of Coke. Tall, pampered, and moneyed, the young tax accountant caught my eye. Of course, he was all over me. I looked *trés* hot in my short, tight, porny little maid's uniform. Don't all rich guys go for the sexy maid at least once in their lives?

I was flattered. But he went for me so attentively and with such great passion, I couldn't help myself. I fell in love with the guy. We quickly built what seemed like a good life.

After it fell apart—so easily, all too quickly—I remembered why I'd been determined to make a life alone, of my own choosing, on my own terms. That's when I started thinking about Ex-Treme Measures again.

Thinking became pursuing, and I developed a plan.

Over the next two years, I worked for a private investigator to obtain the experience I would need to open my own firm. She was a skilled private detective with thirty years in the field, so I learned a lot. Mostly, we handled domestic cases involving extramarital affairs. Mostly, we tailed guilty men to capture on video and in photos what their poor wives already knew in their broken hearts. We shared the results of hours of surveillance, we testified in family court, we tried to help our clients face the reality of their betrayals. So many times, women turned to us and said, "I wish the fucker was dead."

We nodded. We understood. My boss retired. I got my Class C private investigation license and opened my own office in west Deport Beach.

Domestic work was not gratifying. Unfaithful partners tend to behave in the same way, following their dicks until they're caught. Covert camera systems, GPS, and computer software have made tracking adulterers easier than ever before. But when you hand a woman the evidence, there's little satisfaction in watching her weep. That's why Ex-Treme Measures offered something more.

The opportunity to purchase special services was only presented to those who had both the resources and the desire. Word of mouth via the elite underground served as the only form of advertising. Gradually, demand built until there was a steady stream of women willing to pay for ex-tra services. I screened all new clients thoroughly. Only the most appropriate cases were accepted, and only after I completed a thorough period of surveillance and careful vetting. I was extremely selective, and my business continued to grow.

Eventually, I realized I needed someone hefty to help me with the heavy lifting. A discreet strongman with experience in the field and a healthy distaste for the law. Ex-military, ex-cop, ex-con. But without a drug or alcohol problem and without the kind of sexist guile that would get in the way of getting the job done.

The job description was unusual, and the kind of man I was looking for was one in a thousand. It took me months to find the right guy. I couldn't believe it when I met him casually, and he turned out to be the perfect assistant. Ringo was quite the find.

I met him running on the beach. He didn't come on to me, and that earned him a lot of points. Some men build ego just by trying. He had enough without doing that. We worked out together one Saturday, had a couple beers at the Tam. He was looking for work. I was looking for muscle.

At first, I limited his duties to conducting client surveillance. But the truth was, I needed someone to help me with the dead bodies. So one afternoon I invited him to my house after work. I made coffee, and we sat out on the porch while I explained about the special services I offered to select clients.

Secrets are the best aphrodisiac. Ask any adulterer, and he'll tell you it's true.

Maybe that's why we started sleeping together.

Work was good. Ringo was good at work. He was good after work. Ex-Treme Measures thrived.

Until now.

As I approached the turn for my street, I wondered why everything was coming up crap. Was it me? Was I losing the passion I needed to do the job right? Was Ringo right, and it was time to move on? Or was there something else going on?

As I downshifted into the turn, I realized I was at a turning point in my life. It had come to that. Somehow. I wasn't sure why the shit was storming, but there was no denying it was coming down hard.

A fucking nightmare storm of shit.

Chapter Fifteen

As soon as I pulled in the driveway, I knew I'd lost them. The screen door was ajar. The porch was silent. The house sat back on its haunches, stunned, as if it had been stripped, violated, and ruined for life.

I slammed on the brakes and jumped out of the car. I own a registered firearm, which I've never had to use. I have it with me at all times, a licensed concealed carry, but I rarely have reason to remove it from my shoulder bag. However, this seemed like an appropriate occasion to draw my Glock 21, so I did.

When I ran up the front steps, my heart flew ahead and kind of ended up in my mouth. I gagged and tears clouded my vision. My gun hand, however, remained rock steady. As I stepped onto the screened porch, I already knew what I would see. Or what I wouldn't see. Both perches were empty. My babies were gone.

The place was a mess. The room had been ransacked, the rattan couch tipped over, arm chairs upended. Chunks of fruit and seeds were scattered across the Mexican tile. Grey and white feathers were everywhere.

I bent down to look closer. Blood splatter stained the newspapers on the floor.

I wiped away my tears and let out a soft laugh. Drizzled spots of fresh blood provided a trail, one which led from under the perches directly to the front door. I followed the blood inside the house, gun at the ready. I was hoping the birds had pecked the hell out of the intruder. I wanted to find him wandering around blind. I wanted to discover a lifeless body on the floor of the living room, the two parrots sitting together on the back of the couch, preening one another and admiring their handiwork.

The house was silent. A total wreck. Talk about shit storms.

Furniture was strewn about, chairs and end tables upended, the plasma TV face down on the floor. The throw rugs had been flipped back, revealing a surprising accumulation of petty change and dust bunnies. I sneezed as I tiptoed through the ruins of my living room, trying not to crush anything not already smashed to bits. The tears dripped down my face and salted the wound on my lip. There was more blood here and there, but no sign of my birds.

The kitchen cabinets had been emptied out, the contents dumped on the tile. Glass and crockery were shattered, ragged pieces scattered about. I followed the blood trail down the hall to my bedroom. My bed had been stripped, the mattress slashed. The closet and bureau were rifled, clothes tossed around. My underwear lay in a small, embarrassed heap in the middle of the hardwood floor.

The bathroom had the least damage. Someone had swiped almost everything off the shelves, making a colorful mess in the sink. The room reeked of my honey almond shampoo and shea butter soap. Oddly, the amber bottle with the remainder of my antibiotic prescription sat alone on a glass shelf in the top row of the medicine cabinet.

I closed the mirrored door. A lipstick scrawl in old-fashioned cursive, like something out of an old noir movie, provided the following advice from my twisted visitor. *Go Away.*

Funny, that was exactly what I'd been thinking I might do. But now that I was being threatened, now that I'd been told to beat it by such a cruel and destructive force, I decided to refuse to even consider the idea. I wouldn't let some asshat make me run away from my life.

Ass hat.

Who wanted me to leave town? One man came to mind. But I sure didn't want to go there.

By the time I put my gun away, my heart rate had slowed and my blood had chilled. I felt cold, cold inside and out. My beloved birds had been mistreated, traumatized, driven from the safety of their home. This was despicable, unacceptable. War had been declared. Whoever had invaded my home and scared off my babies needed to be tracked down and punished. Would be tracked down and punished. Ex-Treme Measures were called for.

Stepping carefully around my broken belongings, I made my way to the back yard. After burning my shreddings from the office, I dug a hole and buried the ashes. Then I went back inside to deal with the mess, starting with the bloodstains that ran from the porch to the bathroom and through most of what was left of my once cozy, safe, private space.

I saved some blood samples and a few hairs that might not have been mine. Of course, I didn't call and report the break-in to the local police. If what Ashton had told me turned out to be true, law enforcement officers would not be the right people to invite into my life right now. No need to open up any doors I might not be able to close again. But I had my doubts about what my ex had said. It seemed more likely that someone was stalking me. Someone was trying to scare me. It was doubtful my problem was with the Deport Beach police.

As I cleaned my way from room to room, I worked the refuse for evidence. Then I piled the broken parts of my life into a mound of trash. My front yard resembled the infamous mountainous garbage dump in Pompano Beach. The highest peak in South Florida.

It was useless for me to be depressed about the damage. A lot of the furnishings and clothes were remnants of my time as Mrs. Ashton Treme. It would be more productive to look at the situation as a kind of imposed clean slate. I could certainly learn to admire the new minimalism of my interior decor.

Ringo was a minimalist. He would like the way my house looked now. I was tempted to call him, but I controlled the urge. More than anyone, Ringo was invested in whether or not I decided to leave town. I didn't want to suspect him of being a fucked up, sicko manipulator, so I brought out my best mop and scrubbed the floors instead.

Out on the porch, I straightened furniture and swept up seeds and feathers. Then I stood on the steps and called Dr. Trainor. I needed him to remind me how all of us are nothing but animals. I needed him to tell me that destructive behavior, cruelty, and unkindness were all the kind of natural choices animals made. Choices that were embedded in our DNA.

After advising me to leave the door to the porch

open indefinitely so the birds could return home when they were ready, my vet said, "They're traumatized, but there may be more to it. They may be wanting to explore the big world as a couple. This is natural."

I chirped softly in response. If I tried to speak, I might end up weeping. Being alone in that moment was more painful than facing the reality of my love for the two feathered creatures.

Holding the phone to my head, I sank onto the wooden steps and waited for one of Dr. Trainor's evolutionary biology lectures.

Dr. T did not disappoint. "Now that they've had a taste of one another, they may look out in the world for third party options. To compare and contrast, to determine which genetic offerings seem most suitable for their future offspring. The female uses extra-pair copulation as a means for mate sampling. The male feels compelled to spread his genetic endowment far and wide."

Okay.

He snorted. A strange sound, coming from the formal doctor. "Fortunately for you, the availability of viable mates will curtail their desire. The number of African Greys in the palm trees of South Florida is quite limited. Negligible, one might venture. So your pets should return home soon, where the perches are cozy, their food supply steady."

Really? "What about the trauma of being manhandled by an intruder?"

"Their dependency on the food and shelter you provide will overcome any hesitancy to return," he promised.

I thanked him and disconnected, wiping a few tears

from my cheeks. No sense letting my birds' little adventure turn me into a sorry-ass pussy. I propped the screen door open for the birds. Maybe they'd come home once they had their vacation away from captivity. After they either tired of extra-pair sex orgies or discovered they'd been blessed with one another. That each other was all they needed to be content.

Be still, my romantic heart.

When the kitchen floor dried, I made myself a pot of coffee. I pulled up a stool and sat at the counter. Over a cup of Colombian dark—my coffee maker had survived miraculously unscathed—sipped slowly from a gruesome-tasting Styrofoam cup—my coffee mugs had not been so lucky—I began to create a plan. I had to determine who wanted me out of town, and why they were willing to inflict so much senseless damage in order to convince me to leave.

This mess had not been caused by a lack of passion. Or had it?

I made a list and studied it. Then I ripped it into small pieces and went out back to burn the shreds.

****

My phone rang while I was eating Cheerios out of the box. I didn't recognize the number, but I answered anyway. At some point, I would need to return Mrs. Emworth's multiple calls, arrange a time to talk to Mrs. Viscoti Premini, face Ringo before he headed out of town, and deal with my ex. Then I would ex-ecute what I was now referring to in my mind as the final, most extreme measure.

I didn't recognize the number, but I knew it was him right away.

"You got problems again, lady."

"Okay," I said. He didn't know my name. I didn't know his. But I trusted him. This was probably unwise, especially since he reeked of ganja and Budweiser. "Same problem as before?"

"No, but I've been watching your office and someone's in there. It ain't you, right?"

"Right," I said. "You didn't see who went in?"

"It's not the big guy you work with. Your boyfriend."

I wondered how the bum knew Ringo was my boyfriend. Not that he was. Still, were we that obvious? Before I could stop myself, I said, "He's my assistant. I don't have a boyfriend."

Like I wanted to inform the bum of my current availability status. I smacked myself on the forehead. Idiot.

But he just grunted. "So, your *assistant* already came and left, and now somebody else's in there. Want me to do anything?"

"What did you have in mind?"

"I'm out front on the stairs right now. I got buzzed in before. I can make that happen again. Press all the doorbells, somebody'll let me back in."

Some security system. Why were the tenants in my building so stupid? Then I remembered the bike messenger. I hadn't been so careful myself. "Okay, and then?"

"I'll go knock on your door, ask for you. See if that gets 'em to stop whatever it is they're doing. Give you time to get over here."

"Bad idea," I said. "What if they're dangerous? Armed?"

"Lady," he said, "I can take care of myself. Want

me to go up there or not?"

He sounded like he was losing patience. Men can never wait for you to make up your mind.

"You'll want danger pay, right?" I was stalling.

He hung up. Maybe I'd insulted him. I had no idea.

Men. Impossible to figure out and difficult to get rid of. I'd had my fill. It was time for me to find another way to live.

****

When I pulled up in front of the office, a few of the guys from the lot were milling around on the street. I jumped out of my car and rushed over.

"What's the deal?" I asked a short fellow wrapped in a stained bed sheet.

He wore a pair of muddy Army boots held together with duct tape. "Lester has it under control. He told us to wait here and guard the front door. In case anyone tries to escape."

"Thanks." I patted him on the shoulder, and he grinned. His teeth were few and far between.

"He's still up there. With Sammy, a couple other guys."

I thanked him and told the group I would find out what was going on. One of them held the door for me. They were really decent, which depressed me. These guys were alcoholics, addicts, gamblers, unemployed. Most likely they'd all been bad husbands, the bane of their wives' existence. Maybe their women had wanted them dead.

At the top of the stairs, I slowed my run, downshifting into a quiet creep. I slid against the wall, Glock in hand. When I reached the office door, I paused to listen.

Nothing.

I turned the handle and pushed open the door, my gun aimed straight ahead, my heartbeat as steady as my hand. The door banged against the wall, startling the motley group in and around my couch and wing chairs.

Dreadlocks, who apparently was known to his friends as Lester, announced, "Here she is!" He turned to me and said with phony brightness, "Someone's here to see you. He was so anxious to talk to you, he busted in and went through all your stuff."

Papers were strewn everywhere, my desk tipped on its side, the file cabinets dumped on the floor. The room was in such disarray, I barely registered the perp. I let my gun arm drop and walked closer.

My soon-to-be-ex sat cross-legged on the floor at Lester's feet. One of Lester's untied shoes rested on the back of Ash's right hand. If my former husband tried to stand up, my dreadlocked assistant could shift his weight, crushing all those fine patrician bones.

Ashton gave me the most desperate look I'd ever seen on his chiseled face. His bottom lip was bloodied and his cheeks were slashed. In fact, his whole face looked chewed up. He might have been attacked by a gang of hobos, but the facial wounds were not fresh. They were no longer bleeding. I recognized the beak marks.

Ashton Treme had been severely pecked.

My suspicions were now confirmed. The local cops weren't investigating me. Ashton was a liar. And a thief. A stalker. A sick fuck. And a truly bad husband.

The final ex-treme measure beckoned to me like a pint of ES at the Tam.

My blood did not boil. I was calm and cool. "You

guys are the bomb." I walked toward what was left of my desk. The glass was shattered, my computer upside down on the floor. A pointless mess had been made. Like a child had indulged himself in a wild tantrum. Which, in fact, he had. "Catching this bastard in the act. I fucking love you guys."

A fat black man in a pair of overalls gave me the thumbs up from his seat on the couch. The skinny white kid squeezed in next to him nodded and smiled. Lester flashed his dazzling grin. My heart fluttered. Damn heart.

A grizzled old man sat up straighter in one of the wing chairs. "No problem, ma'am," he said. Then he pointed to my ex. "He's a damn pussy, if you'll 'scuse my language."

"He's a pussy, all right," I said, and everybody laughed. They were pleased with themselves, as we all are when we are given a job and we do it right.

"I have more work for you guys, if you're interested." I stepped gingerly around the shattered remains of my desktop computer. "How about escorting this asshole out to the street? You up for it?"

"Vanna, please," my ex whined. "I can explain everything. I know it looks bad and all, but if you just give me a minute I can—"

"Shut the fuck up, Ash." I cut off his phony moan at the root. No more manipulation, thank you. There was no place in my life now for his lame excuses, his empty promises, his spoiled, selfish, and destructive behavior. Being a loser was all he was good for. He had nothing to offer me or anyone else. He needed to be disposed of properly. He deserved to be provided with special services.

After all, the man had failed me as a husband, then taken advantage of me for years afterward. He'd cheated on me, disappointed me, ruined our marriage, our future together. He'd lied to me, begged me for money, manipulated my heart, and messed with my judgment. He'd stalked me, broken into my home, scared off my beloved birds, trashed my office. When I thought about it, I certainly wanted him dead.

I was not powerless. This man did not deserve to be happy at my expense. He certainly deserved extreme measures.

But—

But I just couldn't do it. My heart wasn't in it. Because the truth was, I didn't care anymore. Not enough. Not enough to make the effort and take the risk. Not enough to kill him. I really didn't have it in me anymore.

I was done with bad husbands. I was done thinking about them, tracking their idiotic actions, photographing and exposing their egregious lifestyle choices. I was tired of comforting devastated women who told me nightmare stories about their lying partners, stories that made them fall to their knees and weep. I was tired of the whole bloody mess. Monogamy was a failure, I was a failure, married people everywhere were failures. We were animals responding to our instincts. There was no sense trying to beat that to death. I couldn't kill it off. Nobody could.

Ringo had been right. There were just too many bad husbands. Trying to avenge their behaviors was simply a waste of my time. I was done. I needed to refocus my energies elsewhere.

"That's all I'm gonna take from you, Ashton," I

said.

He cringed. Like he was afraid of me. His wife, the woman whose heart he had gnawed on like the wild beast that he was. "But I can explain. If you just listen."

I turned away. I couldn't bear to look at him, he was so pussified. "You'll stop talking now and not speak another word if you know what's good for you."

I looked at the mess he'd made. The second mess. It was obvious what he'd been after. First at the house, then here in my office. He needed more money to support his habit, much more than I'd been providing with my irregular ATM handouts. He'd been searching for information on my business in the hope of discovering something he could use for leverage. He thought he could blackmail me.

Go Away? A child's way of throwing me off his track.

Which he'd succeeded in doing, but only for a moment or two. I admit it, I did consider other suspects before figuring out what was up. For a few moments, I'd even thought Ringo might have stooped to some below the belt tactics. In order to convince me he was right, that I was in danger. But I knew my former assistant better than that. I felt guilty for even suspecting him.

Ashton, on the other hand, was pond scum. He'd hit rock bottom, then dropped even lower. The man on the floor at our feet was no longer the man I'd once loved. That man was gone. Now this one needed to go.

Lester removed his foot from Ashton's hand and kicked him lightly in the lower back, indicating he should stand up. The four men from the lot surrounded my former husband, grabbing him by his scrawny arms and herding him toward the door.

"I'll be right down, soon as I rescue a few of my things," I said to Lester.

He gave me a deep look. I could feel the blush creep up my neck.

I turned away to focus on the jumble strewn around my filing cabinet, wishing I was immune to the lure of a bad boy. If I wanted to be done with bad husbands, I'd have to eradicate my attraction to bad boys as well.

After the men left, I piled all my files into two metal trash cans, then swept the broken glass into a couple of brown paper sacks from Whole Foods. I boxed up what was left of my computer and cleaned out the desk drawers and the bathroom, packing what I wanted, junking the rest in a large cardboard box I'd stored in the back of the closet. I folded my Donna Karan outfit on top. Then I lugged it all out to the elevator, including the trash, and rode my stuff down to the lobby.

After a few of the guys helped me load up my car, I followed them over to the lot, where Ashton was stretched out on a beat-to-shit Barcalounger. The lot guys had him under guard, and he was still cringing. He brightened at my approach, but his hopeful smile dissolved as he listened to what I had to say.

"It's over. I'm done with you and your problems. I could turn you over right now to the Deport Beach police, and I should. You need to be put away until you clean up. You're a fucking menace. But if I turn you in, what good would that do me? My house is wrecked and so is my office. The cops can't help me there. I could file for a restraining order, but again, what good would that do me?"

Restraining orders never helped my clients. A pile of legal paperwork wouldn't help me either.

"Vanna, please," he begged. "I know I fucked up but we can—"

"Is he still talking?" I asked. Because I'd already stopped listening.

I pulled out the Glock and pointed it at his spoiled, messed up head. The air was still, as if the ocean breeze was cowering, too. Seagulls snowed down from the sky. Some landed in the lot around us. Nobody spoke.

I looked at Lester, who stood at attention behind the ratty lounge chair, waiting. For me to pay him, assign him to do something dangerous or illegal, or maybe just to smile at him. Engage with him. Fuck him. Fall for him. Another man, another psychologically weak man hanging around in my emotional space. Waiting for me to help him make something of his potential. To spur him to action, serve as advisor and muse, boss and voice of authority. Waiting for me to be the person he blames next when he falls prey to bad habits and cheap women, overindulging himself with drink or drugs. Fucking around, fucking up, fucking up my life.

I put the gun back in my leather satchel. I shook my head. I just wasn't that woman anymore.

"Thanks for everything, guys. Let the asshole go. He's not worth it."

Lester raised his dark brows, but he immediately stepped back. He held up both hands and shrugged. "Your call, lady."

Right. My call.

"So fuck off, man," I said to Ashton. "Leave. Now. 'Go Away.' And don't ever come to my house or my office again. If I see you out the window, if I smell your dirty scent on the hot wind, I'll call 911. To report an attempted break-in in progress."

He launched himself out of the easy chair and sprinted out of the lot. The skinny guy tossed an empty beer bottle, which shattered, spraying glass at my ex-husband. He didn't look back. He kept running until he'd disappeared down the street.

The lot guys muttered to one another. I could tell they were disappointed in me. Another pussy woman, not punishing someone who was due for it.

If they only knew.

While I counted out ten twenties to hand over to Lester and the boys, I said, "You men have been extremely helpful today. I really appreciate it."

"Guy's a wimp," the skinny guy said. "We coulda wailed on him a little, made the agenda real clear."

The rest of them murmured their agreement, but Lester said, "Let it go, Sammy. That loser won't be back. He's seen what we can do, and he's gutless."

I nodded. "Too much Oxycontin and Maker's Mark. Believe it or not, that man used to be a powerhouse in a pinstripe suit."

"He's not the only one," Lester said.

I wasn't sure whether he was referring to himself or the members of his peer group in the dirty lot. I handed him the wad of bills. "It's not too late for those of us who still know right from wrong. Good from bad. All that…" I was talking out of my ass, and we all knew it.

"Remember that, counselor, next time you defend some scumbag who's paying you the big bucks to cover his lying ass."

"Yeah," the big guy in overalls added. "Them folks may drive up to the courthouse in fucken limos, but they're no better'n us. Just richer."

I started to protest. Why did they think I was a lawyer? Then I remembered how Ringo and I would stand out in the street, bantering in our lame courtroom jargon. I laughed.

"You guys are one hundred percent right," I said. "You should be running the world."

"That's what we think," Lester said. He wasn't laughing.

As I pulled away from the curb, I beeped the horn a few times. Somebody yelled, "All your objections have been overruled, counselor."

For some reason, this struck me funny. I was still laughing as I drove away.

Chapter Sixteen

When I need to be, I can be vicious and heartless. That's the mood I was in when I returned to my house to dispose of all the things I no longer needed. My hidden minimalist streak shone through, and I liked how that felt on me—lighter, less burdened, more free. I would get rid of my shadows while I was at it. Then I'd fly away.

I turned merciless, dumping almost everything I owned. So much of it had been accumulated during my marriage and the shopping frenzies that accompanied separation, living alone, feeling sorry for myself. I needed so little of what I once thought I wanted.

And there was so much dust. Which is made up mostly of old skin cells, the former you, the past you've shed and not swept up and out. I didn't need that, either. So I divested myself of my former self while paring my life down to the bare essentials.

No more useless keepsakes. No memorabilia. No stupid coffee mugs with stupid quotes on them. No photo albums, no record albums. No handwritten notes and love letters, no old birthday cards, no pictures of us. The blue coral picture frame from our last trip to the islands? Out. The strapless dress I wore to his office Christmas party? Donation pile. The original oil paintings could go to consignment. So could the framed prints. The lamps. The end tables. The throw pillows and throw rugs. Out, out, out.

By the end of the day, you could hear the echo of my footsteps as I wandered from nearly empty room to nearly empty room. I'd get rid of the heavy stuff next or sell the house sparsely furnished. Anything else I no longer had use for would be out on the curb on trash day.

After putting in a call to the local realtor who'd helped me buy the house, I went through my emails, texts, and phone messages. I made a sliced chicken sandwich on whole wheat and a pot of decaf while I psyched myself to wrap up a number of loose ends.

The first call I returned was Mrs. Viscoti Premini's. As I waited for her to pick up, I braced myself for the anger and disappointment in her voice.

"Darling," she said after her personal assistant put through my call. "You've been *so* hard to reach. I've been *dying* to tell you the news."

"Please let me explain why the—"

"Darling, *please*," she interrupted. "You've absolutely no *idea* what you've done for me. My life is my own again. I'm free!"

I picked at a shred of chicken lodged between my front teeth. The meat was old, leftover from a dinner out who knows when. What was she saying? Had her young husband died? Right there on the cold marble floor, bleeding out, convulsing? What happened after Ringo and I left? If he'd croaked, we were screwed. The shower room was probably loaded with hair, prints, fibers. CSI would have a field day.

I sucked in my breath, inadvertently inhaling the chicken shred. I coughed, my heart pounding as I waited for her to tell me what I didn't want to hear, that

I'd killed yet another man who deserved to die. A man who was unreliable, a disappointment, a disloyal asshole, a bad husband. That I'd made her revenge sweet, and she'd be rewarding me in cash. I felt sick. The lump of white meat stuck like a tiny fist in the back my throat.

"He left me *quite* the note," Queen Worth said. "He sounds angry, *very* angry. He blames *me* for what happened. Says he *passed out* in the bathroom after exercising. Says it was because *I'd* been drugging him. For *months*. With the pain medication *I* convinced him to try. To help his lower back injury. The silly boy."

She cackled. I held the phone away from my ear. He'd been on a two milligram dose of Dilaudid for two weeks. All part of the plan for his accidental death. Nothing to laugh at. Yet, Mrs. Viscoti Premini kept cackling. She went on and on, laughing at her own joke. Her own unfunny joke. Why? Because she's one of those smug, self-satisfied people. The kind of people who are pleased with themselves no matter what they do. No matter who they do it to.

"The letter's quite *long* and detailed, and his spelling is *atrocious*. But the dear boy ends his angry note by saying he no longer feels *safe* around me. He's asking for a *divorce*."

"I'm sorry," I said with a short cough.

But really, I wasn't sorry. I was thrilled. The guy was alive. That was enough. I'd lost interest in getting paid. I'd ripped up the retainer anyway. I was done with the case. Now I was free as well.

I cleared my throat. "This was not what we discussed for your situation. It's my fault. Things did not go—"

"Darling, you're *missing* the point. We have him right where I *want* him. *He's* afraid of *me*. The shoe is on the other *foot*, you see. I can kick him to the curb, and he won't *fight* me on it. It's absolutely *perfect*."

The meat bolus shifted a little and slid down my esophagus. I eased it along with a generous swig of decaf. Perfect, eh?

"I guess this *is* good news," I said. "I want you to know your retainer check has already been disposed of. Your fee is settled. Our business is officially completed."

"Don't be *silly*, darling. I want to pay you as *soon* as possible. Ex-Treme Measures *were* taken, and even though the results were not exactly what we expected, they're *extremely* satisfying. *Excellent* work, my dear. A job *well* done. You *must* be rewarded for that."

I sighed. "I'm heading out of town for a bit of a vacation. Perhaps we can discuss this when I return."

I really didn't want to see her. I didn't want her money, either, not anymore. But I had to be professional about the situation. I had to agree to her terms. One of the many things I've learned about rich clients is this—they need to feel like they're in charge or else they'll turn on you. I was cleaning up my business and packing it away. I didn't need anyone flipping on me. My campsite needed to be cleared of all debris and free of smoldering ash.

"I'm willing to accept a small fee for my time and expenses. Let's say, five," I told her. Five thousand dollars was chicken feed to a woman like Dominique Viscoti Premini. But it would satisfy her need to be in charge and effectively terminate our relationship.

"Fine. *Thank* you, Ms. Treme. An envelope with

your name on it will be here, *waiting* for you. Call my assistant when you're coming up this way. So we'll know *when* to expect you."

We hung up without saying good-bye. Ugh. I certainly didn't have any desire to revisit that icky mansion in Palm Beach. Five grand or no five grand, I didn't want to have to relive the worst fuck-up of my career. *Ouch*.

I wanted to call Ringo and tell him he'd been right, the runty boy-toy had made it out of the marble bathroom alive. Instead, I called Dr. Trainor.

As soon as he picked up, I said, "Why do we even try to practice monogamy, Dr. T? It causes us all sorts of pain. Men and women suffer because of something that goes against their natures. Our natures."

He sighed. "Suffering is good for the soul, Ms. Treme. That's why we have religion. Taboos. Laws. Otherwise, we'd stumble from serial harems to sex orgies to utter chaos. Our children would suffer." He paused to let that sink in. "Think about world history. The idea of romantic love is relatively recent. Only since the 1500s have we relied on this particular social system for matrimonial pairing, and it's a system men devised solely to ensure proper inheritance for their heirs. A practical idea that has warped over time. We've fallen in love with the idea of lifelong love. And this is good for civilization, Ms. Treme. The idea of it is good for us. A lofty goal. One we can all aspire to."

A tiny silver feather floated in what was left of my coffee. I fished it out and held it carefully in my palm. So delicate, so perfect.

"I guess," I said. "But all that aspiring causes so much heartbreak."

He agreed. "That it does, but it's also the source of so much poetry. Literature. Music. Art of all kinds. Scientific discoveries accomplished in the name of love. Building of cities and the advancement of civilization and cultural progress. I could go on."

He was right. But that didn't make me feel any better about my own mess of a life.

"Any sign of the birds?" he asked.

"No."

"Be patient," he advised. "They need you."

Maybe. Maybe not. Maybe fuck me.

But I thanked my wise friend and said goodbye.

Sighing heavily, I dialed another client I'd been avoiding. Again, I prepared myself for anger and disappointment. I'd gone AWOL, left Mrs. Emworth in the trenches alone. Or maybe with her driver, I wasn't sure. Either way, I had a job to do and I wasn't doing it. I deserved a tongue lashing.

"Oh, my god," she said when she picked up the phone. "Where have you been? Are you okay?"

I was stunned. This was a first. My clients never worried about my safety. I was like a chauffeur, a necessary means to their own end. A hired hand, someone who would take them from where they were to where they wanted to go. Nothing more. Certainly not someone real enough to be concerned about.

"I'm fine, Mrs. Emworth," I said. "I was undercover on a case and unable to meet you or return your calls."

"Oh, thank god," she said.

I didn't know what to say so I said nothing.

"I needed to talk to you. You said twenty-four/seven, right?" Her voice bubbled hard and fast, occasionally boiling over. I was starting to think I'd been mistaken, that she wasn't concerned for me but for herself. "And I appreciate that, I really do. In fact, I've developed a deep need to talk to you. Because who else can I tell? I have to pretend everything's fine while inside I am sick, sick to death. I mean, I can't take it anymore, the pain, the things he does to humiliate me." Her voice fell to a low simmer. "And I can't tell anyone else the things he says and does to me. Not my daughter, not my girlfriends. Only you. *You.* And you understand, I *know* you do."

That I did. I understood only too well. I wished I didn't. All I wanted to do was hang up. Hang up and eat another sandwich. Drink more coffee. Drink dark beer.

"I wanted to see you at your office to tell you what he did to me. He invited that girl into our home. Our home! And he made love to her in our bed. Our bed!"

I had to hold the phone away from my ear. She was shrieking.

"He knew I might come in at any moment, and he liked knowing that. It excited him, it turned him on. He wanted me to come home that afternoon from shopping and wander into our bedroom and see him fucking that girl on our monogrammed sheets. He didn't care that the help knew what he was up to. He wanted witnesses to my devastation. He wanted to get off on my debasement. He wanted—"

I rolled my eyes. I'd heard it all before. I'd heard it inside my own head, in my own voice. Every moment another emergency, another crisis, another wound forming. *They do it to hurt us, they want to disempower us, they use sex to ruin our self-esteem. They worship us, then stomp on us. They're infantile, evil, out of control, oversexed, screwed up, sociopathic. Listen to what he did next...Blah de blah blah blah.*

I set my cell on speaker and placed it on the counter while I got out the loaf of wheat bread and an old jar of almond butter. The oil had separated and it smelled rancid. I tossed the jar in the trash.

Halfway into a thick peanut butter and mayonnaise sandwich, I heard her winding down. She completed her monologue with a request. The one they all make.

"I want him dead. Why do we have to wait a month? I want that man dead *now*."

I'd heard it all before. So many times. The first few cases I took on were a challenge. Each man was different, with different habits and personalities. Each needed his own personalized death. One that would suit him and not seem suspicious. This required much research, a lot of daring, ingenuity. Back then, disposing of bodies was completely out of the question. I'm fit, but I'm not a man. I couldn't lift the bodies and toss them into dumpsters or car trunks. So I had to find a way to get rid of these unwanted men without having to manhandle them.

My methods were diverse and always ran the risk of discovery. But the wives were complicit, invested in remaining undiscovered. They refused autopsies, invented stories of drug abuse and risky behavior, fainted and collapsed and otherwise distracted with their feigned wild grief when the need for histrionics arose. I trusted my clients, and they trusted me. The Feds had nothing on me. The local police weren't even interested. With the older husbands, the deaths were not unexpected. You'd be surprised what a little extra Viagra can do in combination with copious amounts of alcohol or caffeine. And sex. With the younger men, recreational drugs, booze, and pain meds served as the means to an end. Death by lifestyle is so common these days, no matter what one's socioeconomic status.

Once Ringo came on board, some of my tactics changed. Bad husbands disappeared, never to be heard from again. Others fell off cliffs or out of fishing boats. Once I hired my assistant, the ex-treme options broadened. We also increased the time spent on surveillance. We tried to reduce our risks because now there were two of us to make mistakes. Two of us to suffer the consequences of not being thorough enough.

Because of Ringo, Ex-Treme Measures became a safer business for me to own. We were more professional, our services more comprehensive. He'd even saved me from myself at Queen Worth's. Of course, he was a man. There was that problem. A big problem, one I could do nothing about. But maybe, just maybe, I could overlook it.

Because I trusted him.

Because of what Ringo had seen at the Emworths' estate, because of what he'd told me, because of the fear he felt for our safety, I knew what I had to do. No risks would be taken in the Emworth case. I didn't want to endanger Ringo. Or myself. We had too much to lose.

At least, this was what I was thinking as I swallowed the last bite of nutty mayo. "I think you misunderstood what we can offer you at Ex-Treme Measures, Mrs. Emworth. We are a private investigation firm, licensed in the state of Florida. We can legally investigate your husband's behaviors when he is not with you in order to determine whether he may be having an extramarital affair. And if this seems likely, we can provide you with whatever evidence we are able to capture. Evidence you may need to confirm your suspicions." I sipped my cold decaf. "This evidence is not admissible in court, however. You will need to hire a skilled divorce attorney to advise you on what you might do to facilitate your separation from your husband and to protect your assets. And maximize the settlement. In your favor."

I was running out of steam. I toyed with the little grey feather again, then set it back on the kitchen counter. I was tired of matrimonial distress. Enough was enough.

"Mrs. Emworth, our surveillance has revealed an unsettling complication. It appears that you yourself are having an extramarital affair. Since this runs counter to the case as you've presented it to me, I'm afraid I have to withdraw my services at this point." I took a quick breath and added, "Your retainer fee has been shredded, Mrs. Emworth. I can refer you to some excellent local divorce attorneys if you're interested."

I wasn't at all sure she was sleeping with her chauffeur. Jojo was half her age, married with a new baby. He seemed an unlikely candidate. But she was gorgeous and rich and demanding. Maybe she'd seduced him, maybe they were just friends. I'd never know for sure.

What I was sure about was this—Mrs. Emworth was plotting against us with her driver. She'd enlisted his help because she so desperately wanted to have her husband taken care of via the special services provided by Ex-Treme Measures. Was Mr. Emworth really cheating on her with a younger woman? Ringo had been looking, but he'd found no evidence of that. Mrs. Emworth was so beautiful, maybe her husband had remained faithful. Or maybe they just didn't get along. She was jealous and demanding. Maybe he'd driven her mad years before with his sexual vagrancy, his lack of affection. Or maybe he hadn't done anything but love her and she was after his money. Or maybe she was just plain nuts.

Whatever the truth was, I didn't care. I'd lost interest. Killing off this woman's husband wouldn't solve anything. She needed professional help. There was nothing I could do.

"You have no right to spy on *me*. *I'm* the fucking client. What I do is *my* personal business. I *hired* you. You're working for *me*, and I need you to…"

I shook my head and sighed as she continued her rant. That day she came to my office in tears, hiding her beautiful eyes behind her Gucci shades? I'd thought she was so classy, one of the most impressive clients I'd ever had. I'd been on her side, one hundred percent. What good had all that physical perfection done her? Her wealth, her poise and beauty, had these gifts made her life better? If not, what were they all for?

More ex-istential questions that would remain, for the moment at least, unanswered.

I interrupted her angry diatribe. "I'm sorry, Mrs. Emworth. These are the kinds of things you need to discuss with your divorce lawyer. Please let me know if you'd like our recommendations for local attorneys who specialize in divorce cases. I'd be happy to email you a list."

She was still sputtering and swearing when I hung up.

I was standing before the open refrigerator, studying the near empty shelves and wondering how black olives would taste dipped in expired ranch dressing, when I heard someone out front. On the porch.

My gun was in my shoulder bag. Out front, on the porch.

I tiptoed across the kitchen, listening carefully for the sounds of human activity. I hugged the wall while I crept through the living room. Somebody started talking in a creepy, high-pitched voice.

"Fucking bitch," the voice said. "Bros befo' hos."

I ran out onto the porch.

They sat together on Popeye's perch. "Hello, baby," he said.

I clapped my hands in excitement and relief. "Popeye! You've broken your vow of silence!"

His plumage looked different, his feathers sleek, bright, and full. Maybe the flight, as well as the new love affair, had done my boy some good. Maybe he'd chased some females. Maybe some had bowed to his charms. He'd lived and loved. And here he was, back home with me.

Maybe he loved me after all.

"Tell me," my parrot demanded. "Tell me, baby."

"Tell me, baby," Porsche imitated. I laughed as I closed the screen door. "Fucking ho," she scolded.

"I know, I know," I chirped. "But I'm working on it."

Even though I felt like swooping in and hugging them, I was smart enough not to. I kept my distance. They were pair bonded, and I respected that.

Instead, I grinned and blew them a kiss. Then I

215

went back in the kitchen to rustle up some food for my babies. There is absolutely no truth to the idea that birds eat like birds. They eat a ton of food, their active metabolisms requiring an ungodly amount of calories per ounce of feathers and fluff. Anorexic girls and depressed wives may eat like birds, but real birds eat like horses.

Nature is totally bizarre. Don't ever let anyone tell you that it's not.

****

I had the dream again that night. This time, I ran through downtown Key West. Around Mallory Square. Past the Hemingway House. Then I lifted off and I flew for a long, long time. I soared over clusters of palm trees and drafted on hot winds above the smooth aqua water. It felt so awesome I was grinning when I woke up.

What I needed was a good hard run on the beach. To hang on to my high.

When Ringo rang me up to say he would be coming by, I missed his call. I was out running. So when I wandered up the driveway, stopping now and again to stretch out my hamstrings and calves, the last thing I expected was to see my former assistant sitting on the front porch.

He looked good. Big, dark, sturdy. Like a familiar, comfortable couch. A necessary piece of furniture. One I didn't want to leave behind.

"Hey," he said as I stepped through the screen door.

"Hey, yourself." I was smiling. I couldn't help myself. Especially when I saw the two cardboard cups of coffee. "Thanks," I said when he held out my

Starbucks latte.

I peeled back the coffee lid and tried to act cool. But my heart lurched around like it was half drunk. Which half, the eternal question.

Ringo patted the sliver of couch next to his muscular thighs. "Sit with me for a minute. If you got time for an old friend."

"I've got all the time in the world," I admitted. "I'm client-free. I'm not working on finding any new ones, either. I'm possibly retired."

"I'm retired, too. Thinking about relocating. Key West, maybe. Get away from the Botox mafia."

Key West. What a lovely coincidence. And the Keys were a lot closer than Auckland.

I wanted to hear more about the plan, but Ringo sighed. "There's a problem. Big problem."

I slid in next to him on the couch, absorbing his heat. Inhaling his espresso-rich smell, I leaned on the comfy bulk of my former assistant. When I rested my head against the heart tattoo on his nicely padded upper arm, I swear I could hear that ink beating. The sure throb of his pulse went right through my head down deep in my heart, and it steadied me.

"Does this have to do with two thugs in a black Mercedes?" I asked after a nice mellow pause.

Ringo grunted in surprise. "How'd you... You're always droppin' knowledge on me, Van."

"Not sure that's true. You probably know more than I do. So, who has a problem with us this time? Unhappy client? Criminal attorney? Competitive hitman moving in on our territory?" I recalled the thinking I'd done on the subject earlier, and the notes I'd burned. "I'm guessing the latter." I sighed, snuggling against the sturdy presence of someone who understood. "Never ends, does it? Interpersonal problems, territorial disputes. We're such predictable little animals, aren't we?"

Rhetorical questions, the kind my assistant is used to ignoring. When he shifted in the worn seat and wrapped one thick arm around me, I checked my horniness barometer—hot 'n' humid. I rubbed my sweaty body against my partner. I wanted to preen him, then feed him juicy mango chunks.

"We got issues with those two fucksticks, Van. Big issues." he said softly. "They're from up north, and they don't like what we've been doin' here in South Florida. Or maybe they like it so much, they wanna be the only ones doin' it." His grip on my shoulder tightened.

I reached up and grabbed hold of his hand. We sat like that for a while. The breeze from the east tasted of salt. It ruffled my hair, cooled my hot skin. I liked being in that moment.

Ringo squeezed my hand. Lightly, with love and tenderness. Which felt so comforting, so calming, I felt my heart glide. Like when I run full out down the beach and, about to drop to the sand, I suddenly find the energy I need to keep going. A second wind. That special surge of life force, an innate physiological response. Like all animals experience, at least the ones that manage to survive in this difficult, fucked up world.

"Who do these asshats represent?" I asked Ringo. But what I really wanted to ask him was, *Who do you represent? Are you in it with me for the long haul? One hundred percent?*

Just as he leaned in to kiss me, he said, "Are you

still talkin'?"

I closed my big mouth and offered it to him.

Before he took me on, my man whispered in a low, sexy, boyfriend tone of voice, "They represent a challenge, Vanna. And, knowing you, it's one we're gonna take on."

Which, of course, we did. But that's another story.

Also Available from Mickey J. Corrigan

The Blow Off

Chapter One

My woman of the night career did not get off to a good start, so I decided to diversify. Entrepreneurship, the new black. Since I sucked at sucking dick, I formed a girl gang to seduce and rob rich johns. That was me, being creative and making the best of a badass situation. That's how my crew got started, anyway.

I never would have branched out except the hooker gig was an epic fail from day one. I just didn't have the chops. And you need chops. Most johns want fast head, that's all they're willing to go for these days. Nobody wants to catch a nasty STD, and time is of the essence when you're in a back alley or a parked car. I'm almost six feet tall. I wasn't designed for doing gymnastics in the musty darkness of a leatherette bucket seat.

After the first few hours of the ho routine, my lips went numb. My tongue was totally worn out. It's a muscle, the tongue, and mine had cramps. My chin needed a rest. I had a crick in my neck that wouldn't uncrick. And it was only my first night on the job.

Why oh why did you take out that loan for grad school, Shea O'Grady, I scolded myself as I manhandled yet another slack-dicked stranger. We were in an empty parking lot near MIT, squished into his Ford Escort. The car sucked as much as I did. Why was I always making the wrong decisions? I should have accepted the job offer I'd received from the

Jacksonville public school system, given up my silly dream of becoming a college professor in Boston. What was wrong with me?

As I worked my magic for the brief moment it took to ignite the animal flame inside yet another average chump, a guy too lazy or too stupid or too fucked up to have sex with a loved one, I thought about the mistakes of my life. I'd barely begun to make a mental list when my tenth john of the night exploded with a guttural caveman grunt.

They all sounded alike. Men, getting their rocks off. The more you pitched in to help, the more humdrum it became. I was twenty-five. Was this attitude of mine just a symptom of millennial generation malaise? Or did my day-to-day ennui already include sex? That would be tragic. I hoped the root cause was something else, like my new role as a cheap whore. Or maybe I wasn't cut out for this. Working for The Man. Maybe all sex workers felt like this. How could you like sex when somebody else was hogging the profits?

My musings were interrupted when Mr. John, an overweight businessman in a navy wool suit at least one size too small, grabbed me by the hair. Wow, that hurt. He shoved my head away from his generous lap with a brief review of my work. "Stupid bitch."

Ouch. Muthafuckah, as they say in Boston.

I sat up, said nothing to fat John. Instead, I flashed him an awkward grin. My neck was killing me. Time to cash out for the night, head for the Epsom salts. Outside the dirty windows of the dirty Ford, rain had begun to fall. Buckets of dirty rain. The perfect end to a perfect evening.

It was later, while soaking my neck—and the rest of my body, which felt cold from walking too far in the rain and sore from the heavy paws of strangers—that I suddenly realized exactly how I might deviate from the daily grind. Sitting in the steamy bath, a Heineken in one hand, a tweezered joint in the other, the idea came to me. Fully formed. There it was—a brilliant business plan. A better way to use my skills and youth and looks. I was in hot water up to my chin. Why not add more?

To be honest, I'm not a gorgeous chick. But I am relatively attractive—shiny auburn hair, long legs, and a nice set of perky tits. And I'm practical. So I knew my sex object status was only a temporary window in the long life of a very average woman. Why waste the brief period of seductiveness I'd been given? Wasn't it my god-given right to capitalize on my temporary allure?

Hooking was certainly one way to cash in, but as I had just discovered, not a satisfying one. I wasn't good at it. I doubted I'd get better. My heart wasn't in it. Neither was the rest of my body, apparently. Plus, sex for pay was going to mess up my libido. Hardly seemed worth the aggravation. I massaged my tender neck.

I sucked some good green smoke into my lungs, held my breath, and thought of a better way to use sex appeal to pay my bills. Instantly, I was pumped. My new business idea could relieve me of the burden of nightly blowjobs. I'm no actress. I can look comatose when I'm not mentally engaged in something that interests me. But with a variation on the job description, one that required more intellectual engagement and less drudgery, I might be able to work the gig longer than a single, painful night.

Exhaling a stream of green and feeling so much

better, I had to smile. I now knew what I needed from the whoring biz. I needed to be my own boss. With a crew. Working for me.

Wow. I had leadership aspirations! Who knew?

I snuffed out the joint and polished off the beer. Why work for The Man when you could *be* The Man? Smokey Robinson supposedly said that to Berry Gordy, who went on to found the Motown Record empire. Love that retro music. Those girl groups were killer.

Not too much later, I crawled into bed and, listening to the steady slam of rain against the windows, I drifted off to sleep. I slept well that night and got up refreshed. The sun was streaming in, the blue jays calling out to warn the earthworms of their impending doom. Nature can be so thoughtful.

I brewed up an extra strong pot of coffee. All day, I worked on my business plan.

That night, the second and last of my hooker career, I went to see Cedrick7Z with a business proposition. I was nervous, so I underdressed. Red silk hot pants, white lace bustier, lots of clunky gold, and five-inch do-me pumps with fiberglass heels.

My handler lounged in his usual spot at the John Hancock Jazz Bar, nursing a blue martini. With a strength of purpose and a vibrant confidence I didn't really feel, I slinkied up to the faux leather booth in a dark corner of the softly lit barroom. Then I stood there, heart whirring, until he finally looked up at me.

His black eyes narrowed, pinning me against an invisible wall. I stared back, breathless.

To my relief, the down tempo music helped a little, smoothing out my edginess. Which was essential because Cedrick7Z was going to be a challenge. The

Man was impatient with women. He was also an egomaniac with a notoriously vicious temper. Fortunately for me, my handler had a couple standards. He never fucked around with his sex workers once he'd hired them, and he paid us a competitive twenty-five percent on individual take.

I had to admire the guy. A combination of animal instinct and street smarts had helped launch him from scuzzy gangbanger to pimp alpha dog. In certain parts of Boston—not the nice parts, of course, but the busy and ever-popular scum districts—Cedrick7Z was a powerful man. A man to be respected. And feared.

I gave him a sexy pout and puffed out my chest. Like a robin getting ready to sing for a mate. My heart calmed itself off the ledge with some internal words of reassurance. What was the worst that could happen? The Man would not like my business idea and would order me to go back to playing the skin flute.

"What you want, girl?" Cedrick7Z said, a scowl darkening his baggy, hound-dog face. Your generic pimp, he was duded up in a mint green sateen jacket, signature black leather gloves, and a white angora turtleneck. Two gold hoops dangled from his right ear. "You s'posed to be on the Internet, lookin' for dick."

It was risky, but I made my move. With a quick nod of my head, I sat down directly across from him. I'd worn my hair down, and I let it tumble like autumn leaves around my bare shoulders. He glanced at my cleavage, squeezed just so by my tight top. I licked my thickly glossed lips, fluttered my black paste-on lashes.

When I was sure Cedrick7Z saw just how seductive I could be, I said in my R-rated movie trailer voice, "I have a better idea for what we could do to capitalize on my talents. Give me a few minutes of your time, I think you'll agree with me." I waited until he nodded, then I said, "I have three words for you—seduce and rob."

He grinned. "Go on, baby. I'm listenin'."

Ten minutes later, I had my own blue martini sitting on the white linen tablecloth in front of us. And I was on the verge of sealing a verbal with my handler.

"I like it," he said with a disorienting flash of white and gold teeth. He leaned in, touched my hand. His raccoon eyes showed the whites all around. "But you got to get your own stable, girl, not me. You find the johns you'sef. And you don't let your doin's touch my business. You do all dat, I say, have at it, babe."

He had a good thing going with the local barmen, club bouncers, hotel concierges, and the area cops. He didn't need any bad press to taint his street rep. I totally got that.

When I reached for my drink, he gripped my hand. Hard. *Ouch.*

"I get fitty percent all earnings. Take come straight to me. You and your girls get your pull *after* the merchandise appraised by my guy. Got that, pussycake?"

When I nodded, he let go of my hand. I used my other hand to lift my glass to my slightly trembling lips. I sipped my drink. Oh, that Bombay Sapphire was nice. It had been some time since I'd enjoyed an expensive cocktail.

Smiling now, I said, "If we're going to be business partners, I'd prefer it if you would call me by my stage name. Heaven Scent. Or Ms. Scent, if you're feeling formal."

Cedrick7Z laughed. His gold teeth outnumbered the white ones. "You amuse me, girl. Now get outta here. Go make me some money."

I downed the rest of the martini and licked my lips. Ah, that hit the spot. There would be more of those in my future. My very near future.

Still smiling, I stood up and leaned over my pimp. He smelled like juniper berries and baked potato, not an unpleasant combination. My long thin arm looked especially pale when I wrapped it around his thick, black neck.

"I will make you happy you believed in me," I whispered in his unadorned ear. "Who says men and women can't play on the same team and both win?"

He pulled away, gave me a nasty scowl. "You don't bring me some serious bling by Saturday, it be back to suckin' dick for you, baby. Now go on. I got other business to tend to."

When I fluttered my hand in a queenish wave goodbye, Cedrick7Z just stared at me blankly. I sashayed out of Nectar's as slowly and Marilyn Monroe-ishly as I could.

As soon as I hit the sidewalk, though, I shed my killer heels. Clutching them in one hand, I ran barefoot the four blocks to my car. Shit, man, I had to get a move on. I needed to round up a team to assist me. Pronto. I had to build a crew of hot looking, racy girls. Girls with guts and brains, girls with diamonds in their eyes and a driving urge to take others' tender for themselves. I would have to find two, three, maybe four young women willing and able to take the risk, women who would trust one another enough to form a girl gang. Women who really wanted—needed—and were desperate enough to do this kind of dirty work. They would have to want it as much as I did.

And they had to be available. Right now. Because we had less than five days to pull off our first sexy heist.

The night was overcast but blessedly dry. And warm. Too warm for early June. It was going to be a hot summer in the city. While I unlocked the car, I sniffed at the air. Yum. The magnolias on Comm. Ave. were in bloom. I'd always loved those flowers, their pearly little petals, the gush of sweet scent. Made Boston smell like the long sweet springtimes of the south, of home.

When I gunned the engine, the Mini issued its tiny mouse roar. Laughable. The 1977 vintage automobile sounded like a kid's toy, a joke. But it got me from here to there whenever I was dressed inappropriately for public transportation. Which was becoming more and more the case.

I put her in gear and waited for a break in the traffic, which was incessant and loud.

After my ex-boyfriend went walkabout in Australia and failed to return, I'd kept his car keys, among other items he left behind. The Mini was fun—forest green with racecar stripes and a lot of pep. It was badder than it sounded. The little Britmobile got great gas mileage and was incredibly reliable. In fact, Mini and me got along better than Antoine and I ever had.

Angling out of the space, I poked my square nose into the bustle of evening commuter chaos. I was imagining what my girl gang would be like. We'd be smart vixens, a bunch of super-cool, daringly spicy, wildly tempting babes. Girls who could convince any guy in the toniest club to take them home for some one-on-one time, or some double-the-fun. Girls who would casually slip a man a tongue, a hand job, a mickey, then strip his room, his safe, his jewelry box. Take him on, then take him for all he was worth.

Boylston Street was more clogged than a fat man's arteries. Before I got to the atrial congestion on Mass. Ave., I banged a left, taking the back route home by all the crummy Northeastern University student dorms. Those buildings were in my past now. I'd earn the doctorate in education eventually, but on my own terms. No more sleeping on an air mattress on the floor with the other poor grad students. But no more fifty dollar blowjobs, either. I was going to ride the wave of girl-on-man crime. A budding entrepreneur, I'd grow my stable of foxy cons until we'd taken over the city of Boston. One wealthy sucker at a time.

I was so excited I sang *Happy Birthday* in a breathy voice all the way up Huntington Ave. to the VA hospital, where the traffic finally unclotted with a bloody burst and thinned out to a healthy trickle. I'd given myself a gift, a new moniker, and it was a perfect fit. Heaven Scent was now the handler of a beautiful, ballsy, all-female crew. I laughed. What's not to like about that job description?

While I waited at a red light in downbeat, trashy, but tree-lined Jamaica Plain, I was in the best mood I'd been in since my mother got married. I felt that same sense of freedom wash over me. I was fully independent, relieved of the burden of pleasing someone else. I had my own business! And soon, all my loan troubles would be behind me.

That was the dream, anyway.

About the Author

Originally from Boston, Mickey J. Corrigan lives and writes and gets into trouble in South Florida, where the tropics provide a lush, steamy setting for noir and pulp. The Wild Rose Press is publishing her dark romance series, *The Hard Stuff*. Set in Dusky Beach, each novella in the series focuses on a tough woman in a tough situation who falls in love. Novels include the crime caper romance *The Blow Off* (The Wild Rose Press, Inc., 2015), *Sugar Babies*, a thriller, and *Songs of the Maniacs,* a neo-noir urban crime story.

Visit Mickey at:
http://www.mickeyjcorrigan.com

To chat with Mickey J. Corrigan and other Wild Rose Press authors of romance, join us at www.groups.yahoo.com/group/thewildrosepress.